THE
CRICK CODE

A novel based on the memoirs of a young girl
raised in the FLDS community of Colorado City.

BETSY CLUFF

with BRENDA HOLM

www.thecrickcode.com

This novel is based on the memories of Brenda Holm and reflects present recollections of experiences over time. Some events have been compressed and dialogue has been recreated. Memories have been adapted to move the plot forward as a novel. Most names have been changed, however, a few public official's names have been retained to identify setting. Code of conduct boxes are paraphrased from church meeting notes.

ISBN 13:978-0692190722

Published by Water Rat Productions

Cover by germancreative

For the act of friendship and learning to be your own best friend.

Table of Contents

PROLOGUE: MEETING WITH UNCLE WARREN

MARCH 2002

AGE 18

Uncle Warren's tiny, dark eyes peered through large-lensed glasses perched on his narrow nose as he leaned forward and asked, "How old are you, Becca?"

"I'm eighteen," she whispered.

Eyebrows lifting, he confirmed her worst nightmare, "You're old enough to be placed in marriage." He pulled a small, black book from his pocket and set it on the desk in between them. Opening it, he lifted a pen and wrote her name.

Becca turned icy, and she began to shake.   Just weeks before, the Prophet, Uncle Rulon had placed a girl her age in marriage with a stepfather in his forties. Becca knew it was only a matter of time before the Prophet would assign her to a husband but had held to the hope that somehow the information she had learned in Canada would convince him to give her and Mac a chance.

Even though the forbidden relationship with Mac was what led her parents to set up a meeting with Uncle Warren in the first place, she avoided bringing it up.

"I don't want to marry my Father!" She blurted, surprising herself with the strength and tone of her voice. Had he been the Prophet, she would not have dared speak so boldly.

Uncle Warren turned his gaze to his long, carefully folded hands resting on the black book. As a weapon next to the outburst, he said nothing, creating an uncomfortable, lengthy pause. Pine cleaner scent invaded her nostrils in the cold, sterile office. Portraits of former Prophets lined the walls and she felt like she was being watched.

Seeming satisfied with the silent pause, he looked at her again and calmly asserted, "That doesn't happen unless the girl requests it. It has to be approved by the Prophet and Heavenly Father through revelation."

His controlled voice took her back to the Alta Academy where she had first heard him during daily devotionals as a young child. In those days it was all she knew, a noise in the background. Now it was the most evil sound she could imagine.

Since when did a girl have the right to request anything? And the Prophet, Uncle Rulon? He hadn't been seen in weeks. Faithful leaders were being advised by Uncle Warren that the Prophet would only recover to his full strength from his stroke if the people would just repent of all their sins and deal with their own weaknesses and impurities. That way, Uncle Warren would only have to channel his Father's voice a little longer.

Becca was beginning to seriously doubt he would ever recover, even though he had just gained more wives. The last time she had seen him, he could barely even say the words, "keep sweet," without drooling.

Besides, Becca knew for a fact that the girl had not requested to marry her own stepfather. It just didn't make sense that Uncle Warren would say such a thing.

Tears pooled in her big hazel eyes. Hating to cry in his presence, she willed them back. Powerless to change generations of teachings handed down, she wanted to shout her thoughts but sat paralyzed instead.

Her ideas could not stand against the words of the Prophet, the code of the Crick that demanded absolute obedience and promised a superior existence to anyone who followed. If superiority meant giving up her right to make choices in her life, then she didn't want it.

Uncle Warren stood and slid a box of tissues to her hand. It seemed like a kind gesture, but one with an ulterior motive. He had a way of putting her in her place to make her feel small, like a child.

"I don't want to marry someone I don't know either!"

She had to say it. Even if it made no difference, she had to at least try, for her own sake, to have a say in her future. Holding another man's hand and being sealed for all eternity like her sister was…without a voice, and without a choice was not what she wanted.

He turned his back to her and looked out the window, then responded coolly, "Do you not trust the Prophet?"

What could she say? If she said yes, or no, it didn't matter. Her words meant nothing.

"Yes," she replied in almost a whisper, knowing it was the only answer she could give that wouldn't go against the Prophet.

They sat in silence. Becca wondered how many girls had suffered in the same chair under the same circumstances. Surely she wasn't the only one.

"Go home and pray to receive guidance and peace. You need to trust the Prophet and your Father." He paused, and then added, "If you were to be with that boy, you would never be happy. If he is seeking you out, then he has impure thoughts."

Their relationship had gone way beyond thoughts months before, but Becca wasn't about to tell him that.

"Would you like to go out the back door?" He asked. It was an odd question. He must have known her mothers and Father were waiting for her in the front sitting area. It was like he wanted to seem like a hero. Becca didn't want to face everyone else with her swollen eyes and red nose, so she nodded and walked to the door.

To her back, he said, "Any boy who seeks a girl cannot be trusted. He will be asked to stay out of town and may lose his priesthood."

Becca turned to face him. He walked to her and gently lifted her hand, cradling it between his clammy, cold fingers. Looking into her eyes, he said, "You must remember, Becca, you are a chosen daughter of Zion. Your heavenly Father loves you, and you must trust the Prophet. He knows what is best for you."

Pulling free, she turned lifeless to the door, opened it and walked outside to think.

Crap! Did Mac lose his priesthood?

Her whole life felt as if it were slipping away as she stood paralyzed, her back to the door on the stoop of the Prophet's home.

Every fear she had known for the last two years was unfolding. Ashamed, she remembered boys she had judged as apostates. They were not allowed to return, and now Mac was one of them.

She was done. Done trying to please the Prophet. Done trying to follow the rules. Done trying to ignore her own heart. She had to contact Mac and let him know. That would be impossible from home with her three mothers and Father eying her every move. Any phone call would draw attention to herself and her intentions. Remembering a phone in an office at the Spud Pit, she decided to go there first rather than a friend's house or work. She could not risk anyone hearing what she was about to say.

Wishing Father had not taken her bike, she pulled her coat tight as the March, mid-morning wind whipped around her face and she walked toward the Spud Pit. No doubt, her parents would be confused as to her whereabouts, but probably would assume she was walking to work.

Hardening herself to the reality of what must be done, she pushed forward. This time there would be no turning back. She had walked the same streets to secretly meet up with Mac under the shelter of night dozens of times.

It was daytime, though, and there was nothing that could shelter her from what she had to do. Uncomfortable with the sunlight, she closed her eyes and continued to put one foot in front of the other, refusing to let fear settle. It would not serve her where she was going. Her whirling thoughts settled onto one aching question.

How has my life come to this?

And with every step, she remembered.

1

BEFORE THE CODE: RIVERTON, UTAH

1992

AGE 9

CODE OF CONDUCT: OBEDIENCE

You must obey the priesthood over you. To do this, you will have to give up your own will and sacrifice your own feelings. You must keep sweet, no matter what.

Lifting her chin and closing her eyes with satisfaction, Becca stepped out of Grandmother's station wagon and walked the short distance home alongside her siblings, determined to enjoy the rest of the day away from sitting still at school. Begging to be breathed, the crisp, fall air enticed, and the warmth of the sun dared her to join the dance of the real world. All she wanted was to put her school bag away, eat a snack, and have some fun.

"Come on guys, let's go do somethin'!" Becca urged as she dropped her book bag on the counter, grabbed two big, fat homemade cookies, and walked toward the front door. How anyone would want to sit inside was beyond her.

After being cooped up at the Alta Academy all day, that was the last thing she wanted to do. Learning reading and writing was mostly fun, and she liked the ride to school with her cousins and Grandmother.

However, each day she faced the uncertainty of being called on during seminary and questioned about her scripture reading. That was enough for her to not like school at all. At the end of the day she had enough energy stored to go to the moon and back.

One of the perks of having three brothers, two sisters, and a couple of cousins living next door was that there was always someone to play with. Most days they would grab a snack and then head outside to rollerblade, ride bikes, or explore.

She knew children down the street who would go inside and sit in front of the television until bedtime. That was not her idea of fun. Not that she had anything against TV. The once-a-week funny home video show her parents would let them watch was one of her favorite activities, but this day was no movie day.

After waiting a few minutes with no response from her siblings, Becca moaned and started for the door, "Fine, I'll just find someone else."

Ted, her oldest brother, swaggered down the hall with his skinny, long legs. She would bet her braid he was walking like that just to make her mad. He liked to make her angry, and then act innocent.

"Chill out, Becca, I'm comin'," he said.

"Me too." Benjamin, her twin brother, joined in as he fumbled to re-tie his shoes he had just kicked off. He wasn't moving slowly to irritate. He was just slow and deserved patience. Ted deserved a pinch.

Eyebrows lowered, Becca opened the door and started to slam it, but left it open just enough, hoping they didn't change their minds.

Minutes later Ted, Tilly, and Benjamin joined her on the porch.

"How 'bout rollerbladin?" Benjamin suggested.

"I wanna play hide-n-seek in the hay," Becca announced.

"Sounds good to me," Ted agreed.

"I don't want to get all dirty. Besides, Benjamin can barely breathe in the hay," Tilly countered.

"I breathe fine in the hay," he said as he looked up through smudged glasses.

"He's not sick right now. He'll be fine," Becca said.

Benjamin nodded his head in agreement with Becca, and Tilly was outnumbered by them, three to one.

"Last one to the stacks is 'it!'" Ted challenged and ran ahead.

Tilly sighed, paused with hands on her hips, and then started to run so she wouldn't be "it."

Lighthearted, Becca skipped as her hair bow blew off to the side, and her long, pink dress flew in the wind. Hide-and-seek was so much fun to play in the stacked hay. It was a maze that hid all sounds. Breathing quietly, a kid could disappear for hours without being found. None of her siblings could do it. A fit of giggles would always take over once someone was close. But it was a challenge, and Becca loved it.

Even though Tilly pranced and held her dress like a queen, Benjamin was last to the stacks. He would be "it." Becca felt guilty. Benjamin was always "it" first because he was slower than the rest of the children. One time she had overheard her Mother explaining to an Aunt about when they were inside her mother's belly, her mom's body started to do weird things. Somehow it affected Benjamin, but not Becca. That made her feel bad too, but she couldn't do anything about it, so she tried not to think about it too much.

"One, two, three…" Benjamin counted as bodies scurried off into the maze. Ted was the first to disappear. Once again, Tilly lifted her skirt and pranced away. Becca darted past her sister and ran far into the musty maze. She shot ahead of Ted who was crouching behind three stacks and continued deep into the field, determined to win. All sounds were wiped out by the tall, yellow-green towers.

Slowing to a walk, she found the perfect hiding spot where someone had placed several bales together to form a cube with a hole in the middle at the top. She climbed and lowered herself into the hole. It was too dark for her to see after being out in the bright of the sun.

Restless from the run, she tried to inhale and exhale slowly. Exhaling was the easy part, but the thick, urine-like smell of the hay made it hard for her to inhale. Uneasy, she comforted herself by twisting the tip of her braid in her fingers.

Once her eyes adjusted, she realized someone had been there before her. It made perfect sense that someone had been there. Someone had built it after all. Nestled in the corner, she could see candy bar wrappers and some kind of book. Inching toward the items, she lifted the glossy-covered paper and realized it was a magazine. Educational books and Church Scriptures were the only reading materials acceptable in her house. Magazines were not.

A woman's chest, covered only by folded arms, stared back at her. A sick feeling gathered in her belly, and all her excitement for the game was lost. She forgot the challenge, the air, the sun, and even her breath.

Her hands held a picture of a naked lady. *What the heck?* Looking away, her whole body turned hot, mortified. As early as she could remember, she had been taught that a body was sacred, and no one was allowed to see it. Embarrassed to be naked even by herself, let alone see someone else, she was horrified, but still couldn't resist the curiosity to open it. More skin than she had seen all her life greeted her as she turned the page. It was a man.

A snake!

Principal Jeffs had warned every day at the Alta Academy that girls were not allowed to even think about them. Aside from her brothers, Becca had never, ever seen a boy's skin under their chin. Her mouth dried up, and her hands felt as if they weighed more than a big fat watermelon. Throwing the magazine, she readied to climb out of that nasty place.

Distracted by the magazine, she hadn't noticed that her brothers and sister were just at the base of her hideout. Just as she poked her head above the hay, they yelled, "Gotcha!"

She scampered out. Her braided, honey-brown hair was raised with static electricity and puffed in all directions. Pushing past her siblings, angry more because of what she had seen than the act of being caught, she said, "I'm done playin'." Wringing her hands, she tried to erase the presence of the magazine.

"Awe, Becca, don't be a sore loser," taunted Ted as he followed behind. "You're the one who wanted to play, so let's play."

"You can't just say you're done after one time," Tilly argued.

"Come on Becca. I'll be "it" again," Benjamin offered.

The free spirit she ran with into the maze disappeared. All she wanted to do was get home, wash her hands and wipe the images from her eyes.

"I'm *not* a sore loser. I just. I just. I just saw somethin'!" Becca countered, motioning towards the hay.

"Oh, that's kinda cool! It's like a house," Ted said as he hiked his body onto the structure and lowered himself inside before Becca could distract him.

"Who's been eatin' candy? Oh, what's this?" Ted said.

Seconds later his head popped up, and he was holding the magazine. For a few moments, no one, not even Tilly, said a thing as Ted stepped down with it opened for all to see.

"That's gross!" Tilly shuddered, "We shouldn't look at that!"

They all knew they shouldn't look at it, but even Tilly took another glance before she turned and huffed off toward home.

Benjamin's cough worsened, and his thick glasses steamed.

"Come on Benjamin, we gotta get back before you start coughin' too much," Ted said, throwing the magazine back into the hole, and the two boys followed as Becca stomped toward home. Thoughts ran wild inside her head.

Why'd anyone read a magazine like that? Why'd it be inside a hay-field house?

Her hands felt itchy, and all she wanted was to give them a good scrub as if somehow it would take away the filth of seeing an almost-naked body.

How could a picture like that be taken, let alone put on the cover of a magazine for everyone to see? The only time a person took off all their clothes was when they took a bath. It made no sense. At her house, during the summer when the pool was set up, everyone even wore clothes while swimming. That was the natural thing to do. Except when she took swimming lessons at the community pool before getting her longies, Becca always swam in her clothes.

Lost in thought, Becca looked up as they approached the dirt road. Dust was rising, and a familiar pink and white van was racing down the dirt road. Dust pooled all around as Mother stopped the van right in front of them. Immediately Becca hoped Ted would just keep his mouth quiet about the dirty magazine. They hadn't had time to talk about whether or not to tell their parents. If Mother found out about the magazine, she would want to talk about it, and talking about the horrible picture would just make it worse. Ted opened the van door, and they noticed Mother had already picked up Tilly. Justin and Janessa, her two youngest siblings, were also in their car seats fast asleep.

"Get in quickly," Mother ordered and then started to drive before the door was all the way closed.

Shocked by their mother's odd behavior, they obeyed without a fuss. Becca looked at Justin and Janessa to see if they were injured or sick. They looked fine enough.

Outside the house, the van jerked to a stop. Before getting out, Mother gave them strict instructions. "We're goin' to the Crick tonight. Grandfather's on his way to get us. We're goin' without dad. Now go in and pack."

Becca looked at her sister and mouthed silently, "Without dad?"

Tilly looked back with a blank stare and started to unbuckle Justin and Janessa. She didn't know either.

With a wobbly smile, Mother lifted her hand to wipe her forehead, looked at the children through her rearview mirror, and then said, "Just leave the young ones to sleep, Tilly. Pack for 'bout a week, we gotta be gone before dad gets back."

Scrambling to her room, Becca obeyed blankly, not knowing what to bring or how long they would stay at the Crick. Paralyzed by questions, she knelt in front of her dresser motionless.

"Pack, Becca. Mother said to hurry," Tilly rushed, cramming her tote full of clothes.

"But I don't know what to bring."

"Stop thinkin'. Just pack," Tilly said grabbing clothes from Becca's drawer and stuffing items into her bag violently. "There, you're done. Now come on."

"I gotta think," Becca said, grabbing her bag from Tilly. "Tell Mother I'm almost done."

Without a word, Tilly turned, growled under her breath and left the room.

Scanning her dresser, Becca reached for some colorful pens, her hairbrush, and a notepad then barreled down the hall without looking back. Grandpa John had arrived. It was time to go.

***

As the only home she had ever known disappeared behind the trail of dust that shadowed them like a storm, Becca stared out the back window of her Grandfather's van. Desiree, her cousin, waved quizzically from her front yard as they passed.

"Stop! Mother, tell Grandfather to stop. We gotta say bye to Desiree," Becca urged and pressed her face to the window.

"We can't stop today, Becca. We have to get goin'."

"But she's outside…" By the time Becca reacted and waved back, the van was already too far away for Desiree to see. As long as Becca could remember, she and Desiree had been best friends. Not one holiday or birthday went by without her company. They were double-cousins and proud of it.

"But Mother, Desiree will wonder about me. We can't just…"

"Enough, Becca, we gotta go. You can write her a letter," Mother urged with a forced smile.

Where Mother could not see, Tilly shoved Becca's shoulder and mouthed silently, "Stop buggin' mom!"

Against everything her heart was telling her, Becca closed her mouth, stared out the window, and noticed her chest pounding as if her heart were trying to escape.

What just happened? Why was Mother in such a hurry? Why are we leaving with Grandpa John?

Lifting her hand to wipe her forehead, she smelled the faint, musty odor of hay and remembered the magazine. A new kind of shame and fear filled her as she looked down and saw two filthy hands. In all the chaos, she had forgotten to wash.

2

A NEW HOME: THE CRICK
1992-93

CODE OF CONDUCT: APOSTATES

To turn against the prophet is the worst thing a person could do.
They will become an apostate and suffer.

Grandpa John drove the whole way, and except for occasional, whispered conversations with Mother, he kept to himself. Every once-in-a-while, Mother turned around to check on the children with a reassuring smile. Exhausted from the shock of the afternoon, Becca stopped thinking and fell into a restless half-sleep.

Just before they turned off the main road, Becca woke and wondered if she had dreamt the whole thing. That would make more sense than anything. If it was a dream, then she hadn't actually seen a dirty magazine, they hadn't left dad at home, and she hadn't missed saying goodbye to Desiree. But as her brothers began to bicker, she looked out the van window and saw familiar territory. It wasn't a dream. They were at the Crick.

Wooden-sided, half-finished, two-story homes littered the land, and she wondered why those houses never seemed to get done. The Crick was nowhere near as tidy and finished as Riverton, but the natural landscape was breathtaking. Dusk was settling, wrapping the horizon with rosy pink and orange colors reminding Becca of Grandmother's crocheted blankets. Everywhere Becca looked she could see another red-rocked hill to climb and couldn't help but feel peaceful, despite what had happened earlier.

"There's Cottonwood Park," Tilly said.

"There's my big tree," Ted added.

"Ohhhh, I like that tree," Justin chimed in, and Janessa squealed.

Trips to the Crick were usually fun. She remembered family gatherings celebrating the Prophet's birthday, harvest fests, church conferences, and grandparents' birthdays. Each event was filled with home-made foods and goodies sold from booths at Cottonwood Park. Outdoor barbecues loaded with chicken legs and corn-on-the-cob would be fired up as colossal cottonwood trees stood soldier-like overseeing the festivities. Wider than most cars, the trees had been there since Becca's mother was a little girl. Every child for generations had probably climbed the friendly giants.

"Are we almost there?" Justin asked.

"Just about," Mother answered.

The Crick was made up of twin cities: Hildale and Colorado City. Hildale was on the Utah side while Colorado City was on the Arizona side. Neither was much of a city, but that was what they were called.

Grandpa John's house was a familiar, happy place Becca liked to call the "Red Rock" house. Located on the Hildale, Utah side of the Crick, it was situated right in front of a lovely hillside under the most beautiful red rocks where she and the other children could play and hike for hours.

Two of Grandpa John's four wives lived in the "Red Rock" house which was made up of two identical homes stacked one atop another. Each wife lived on their own level. Grandma Leah lived on the upstairs level and Becca's blood Grandma, Claudia, lived on the lower level. They were blood sisters but were different as night and day.

Everyone in both cities practiced polygamy. Becca knew her family believed in the practice and accepted it as normal, even though her dad had only one wife. She had many cousins with one dad and several moms. While some families in their Riverton neighborhood did not practice polygamy, at the Crick, everyone did.

A man with at least three wives was a good thing; she knew several families with more than three mothers. Sometimes Becca envied those large families and even imagined what it would be like to have more than one mother and extra sisters to play with.

As they approached Grandpa John's house, the younger children started to wake. For the first time since their hasty departure, Becca began to feel excited to see her Grandmas.

As if she could read Becca's thoughts, Grandma Claudia, already dressed in her nightclothes with her unspun graying hair hanging down one shoulder, opened the front door and walked out as the van pulled up. She had a smile on her face, but her eyes were dark and thoughtful.

Tilly got Janessa from her seat, and Ted opened the van door. One by one the children jumped out.

"I'm so glad you came to visit," Grandma said as she kissed each one on their heads.

The children took turns giving her hugs and then grabbed their suitcases. Somehow Becca knew this was not going to be an ordinary visit.

***

"Dad's here!" Becca squealed and threw Ted's bike down as she ran to the gate to greet him by his car. It had only been a few days since she had seen him in Riverton, but it felt like weeks.

Happy hollers echoed off the canyon walls, and the other children scurried out to join them, throwing out questions like water balloons.

"Are you stayin'?"

"Did Desiree ask about me?"

"Are you takin' us back to Riverton?"

Mother stood straight-faced in the entryway and watched it all unfold.

"Children, I need to talk to your dad," she said gently.

Reluctantly, the children let him go and headed to the backyard, keeping them in eyesight so they could watch and try to listen. Becca lifted

Janessa into a wheelbarrow and pushed her around, so she could get closer while keeping the appearance of play. Dad looked angry and sad at the same time. Mother tried to keep a smile and talk in a quiet voice.

After a short while, Mother turned and waved the children back.

In an instant, they all ran over and continued bombarding them with questions.

"Can he eat dinner with us?"

"You stayin' the night, dad?"

"Dad's here just for a day visit," Mother said.

"How about we go for a hike at Maxwell Park?" He suggested, looking at their mother.

"You can go for a hike, but I'll stay here with Janessa and Justin," she said.

Excited to be with him, the children jumped at the idea and scurried to gather water bottles and jackets.

"Come on, Dad, I want to show you somethin'," Becca said, motioning toward the house.

"Dad's not comin' in, Becca," Mother said and walked inside.

Becca followed her in to fill her bottle. "Why can't dad come in?"

"Not right now, just go along and have fun," Mother said and went to the kitchen sink to wash dishes.

***

Maxwell Park was a beautiful oasis of green grass and trees. Directly behind the grassy area was the best-hiking mountain at the Crick. It was one of Becca's favorite places in the world. Delighted to be able to share it with her dad, Becca hung around the car as Benjamin and Ted ran ahead, and Tilly followed to make sure they didn't get into trouble.

Wanting some answers, Becca stayed close to her dad as they walked to the hiking path.

"Have you seen Desiree?"

"She came by and asked about you. I told her you were visiting Grandpa John and Grandma Claudia."

"Tell her I miss her."

Dad smiled and said, "I'll do that."

"When do we get to go home?" She wondered.

"I'm not sure," he answered.

"Why not?" Becca questioned. It seemed weird that he couldn't just tell her. He was her dad. Dads could decide those things.

"Well, the Prophet has said you children and Mother need to be here for a while."

"Are we in trouble?" Becca asked, remembering the magazine.

Could the Prophet have known about that? He knows everything, maybe he knows.

She had seen the magazine just minutes before her mother came to gather the children that day, though, and the Prophet had already told Mother they were to leave.

"No. You're not in trouble. You kids are here with Mother so I can get some things in order back in Riverton," he assured.

"So, after that, we will come home?" she asked searching for something concrete.

"Hopefully. Hey, we didn't come out here just to talk. Let's hike!"

They explored for hours, and even though Mother stayed home, it was like the whole family was together again.

But after returning from the hike, since her dad wasn't allowed to go inside Grandfather's, they all hugged good bye and Becca stared at the back of his car as he drove away.

That evening, Becca crawled in bed and overheard her mother crying in the next room. Straining to hear, she figured mother was on the phone with dad. She heard something like, "I wish we could get back together, too. I love you, too. We have to pray and ask for an answer; I have to do what the Prophet says until you can get your priesthood back."

Becca thought that was just plain stupid. If Mother loved Dad, then they should be together. Besides, her dad already had the priesthood.

Why'd Mother say he had to get the priesthood?

Instant guilt washed over her for questioning Uncle Rulon, the Prophet, by thinking something he said was stupid. When a person doubted the Prophet, they showed a lack of faith. If one wanted to "Keep Sweet," then they had to fight the urge to question. Becca had known this fundamental truth as long as she could remember and vowed to do better.

She tried to sleep. That didn't work, so she closed her eyes and pretended the whole family was together again in Riverton. Fun memories like roller-blading on the carport with Desiree or playing in the snow in their front yard comforted her. A few times her mind wandered to the last time they had played hide-and-seek, but quickly changed to something else. Trying to keep focused on one thing, Becca decided to think about their last Christmas together.

A light-covered ten-foot-tall tree had towered over what seemed like hundreds of presents on the floor as Becca, and her siblings rushed downstairs. The older kids sorted gifts into piles as their mom caught it all on videotape. One by one, they opened plush blankets, baby dolls, and books. It was like watching a show as dad opened his presents. He acted goofy, making noises and faces like he was advertising on a TV commercial. Fits of laughter from the children would burst forth as mother said, "Oh Travis, stop bein' a tease."

When they were all exhausted after a day of playing with new gifts and stuffing themselves with Christmas food, they all knelt to pray. Dad asked Benjamin to say the prayer. Quiet groans escaped from the older siblings. Everyone knew when Benjamin prayed it took forever. He had to think and then talk. Why Dad would pick Benjamin, Becca couldn't guess. But they all knelt up tall, closed their eyes, bowed their heads and waited. And waited. And waited. Trying to keep her balance, and anxious for the prayer to be done and over with, Becca slowly opened one eye to somehow hurry Benjamin along. Without hesitation, a large, dad-finger came whirling towards her guilty eyeball. Becca swerved, almost falling over, and then closed her eyes tight, just as Benjamin began to speak...

Just thinking about her dad made her feel better. As she recalled the whole scene, she concluded that he must have chosen Benjamin on purpose just to have fun by poking eyeballs. He always knew how to have fun.

Her mind wandered to school. Becca was used to the Alta Academy in Salt Lake. Grandma Doris, Dad's mom, was the librarian there and had also been their ride to school. Every day, with aunts, uncles, and cousins in the station wagon, they had driven to the Alta Academy built on the Jeff's compound. Upon arrival, all students met in the main room where they also had church on Sundays. Principal Warren Jeffs led a daily devotional every morning, and the children were given advice on how to keep sweet. He talked as slow as a snail, but at least he wasn't scary like her new teacher at the Crick. Mr. Ferber was a fat, bald man with a deep, booming voice that made her shudder each time he said her name. Even though she had only been in his class for a few days, she almost peed her pants twice, afraid to ask him if she could be excused to the restroom.

In between all her thoughts, Becca begged her body to go to sleep. There was just no way to figure out the dad thing, the school thing, or *anything*. As hard as it was, she needed to turn her head off and get some rest. It was Saturday night which meant church the next day. It was torture to stay awake during church if she didn't have enough sleep the night before.

***

Classical music and the aroma of coffee filled the house as the children hustled to get ready for church. In between piano and string sounds, Becca could hear Janessa squealing as Tilly combed and braided her hair. Happy chatter floated in from the kitchen and Becca recognized uncles' voices. Every Sunday Grandpa John's house was the gathering place for the whole family. Grandmother Claudia would bake coffee cakes and enjoy coffee with her children and grandchildren. If she weren't so tired from the lack of sleep the night before, Becca would have already been up enjoying the cake and conversation.

Instead, she dragged her sleepy head off her pillow and started to get ready. Donning her longies, leggings, pantyhose, and dress took her a while. If something was crisscrossed, it felt uncomfortable and would bug her all day, especially the longies. Jumpsuit-like underwear just wasn't comfortable.

She had received them after being baptized when she was eight at the Alta Academy. From that point forward, she was expected to wear the protective clothing. Only her neck, head, hands, ankles and feet could be seen when fully clothed. While it was exciting at first to wear the holy clothes, Becca found them stifling and sometimes didn't wear them. In Salt Lake she could get away with such disregard, but not at the Crick. People noticed that sort of thing at the Crick.

Before gathering her bag filled with notebooks, scriptures and colorful pens, Becca looked at her reflection in the mirror. She was tired. It was going to be a long day.

Church meetings were somewhat the same as in Salt Lake except for the meeting house in Colorado City was much fancier than the Jeff's compound. Nestled next to another red-rocked pocket of stone guarding the valley, it was an impressive, white building. On Sundays, it held meetings for hundreds of faithful followers. Just like in Salt Lake, Becca and her family would sit for up to 4 hours listening.

"Children, we gotta hurry, so we won't be late," Mother called from the kitchen.

It won't be the first time, Becca thought.

She didn't like being late either, but if they were late, at least they didn't have to sit so long.

"Becca, come on, you haven't even eaten yet!" Tilly scolded from the bedroom door.

Without a word to her sister, Becca walked past and into the busy kitchen. "Here," Mother said as she sweetly placed a piece of coffee cake in Becca's hand, "eat it in the van. We have to go."

With that, everyone filed out the front door. Just before climbing into the van, Becca remembered she had forgotten to put something in her bag. Quickly, she jumped out and ran into the house as protests and accusations rose from her siblings in the van. Ignoring the scolding, Becca ran and retrieved a bright red package she had been saving all week, then scampered back and buckled up.

"We're gonna be late now."

"Everyone's gonna look at us."

"Leave Becca alone. Next time she'll be better prepared," Mother voiced as she drove.

Church had already started. That meant they would have to sit on the hard chairs towards the back. Tilly threw Becca a this-is-all-your-fault stare as Mother and the others filled the seats. It was done. They were there. Now came the hard part of sitting and listening as "Uncles" gave talks. Thank goodness Becca had her bag full of goodies she needed to sit through hours and hours of talks. Today she had a secret weapon. The red package. Carefully she opened a notebook, chose a purple pen and began to write.

Proud of her abilities to take good notes, Becca wrote almost every word as monotone "Uncles" delivered messages at a snail's pace. She had to keep writing just to stay awake. Sometimes a whole page would be filled, and Becca didn't even pay attention, but the words were there.

Some words were hard to spell and others she didn't even know the meaning. But still, she wrote.

> *"The priesthood doesn't leave you; you leave the priesthood. There is no protection outside of the priesthood. If a man does not hold the priesthood, then the family is not protected from evil. Armageddon is near; there is no time left. Everyone is going to have to look at themselves and see if they have kept sweet..."*

The speaker continued, but Becca stopped writing.

Mother had said something on the phone about dad getting the priesthood just the night before. Hearing it in church was different. Did Dad leave the priesthood? But he was a good dad. He wasn't about to let evil get his family. Becca felt torn.

Did dad do somethin' wrong for the Prophet to take away his priesthood? The speaker made it sound like dad chose it.

It was too much to think about, and Becca had lost her place, so she put her pen down. Needing a distraction, she fiddled in her bag to find the colorful, red package.

Grasping both sides, she tore the package carefully to avoid making any sound. However, before she could even react, the bag quickly gave way, and colorful candies flew, raining down like tiny basketballs on the hard, marble floor. Squeezing her eyes shut, Becca froze, gripped her now almost empty candy package, and wished she could turn back time.

Heat rose through her body up to her face. Heads turned as several children discreetly scooted their feet to gather the red, green, and yellow candies that were supposed to be Becca's distraction. All she could do was sit still, smile softly and pretend it didn't just happen.

To her left, she heard a heavy sigh as Tilly tilted her chin the opposite direction. Ted snorted and reached discretely for a piece himself. Benjamin looked at her with compassionate puppy-dog eyes and Janessa giggled. Mother was so focused on the speaker, she didn't even notice.

3

LEARNING THE CODE: A NEW KIND OF NORMAL

1993

CODE OF CONDUCT: GUILT

When you shake his hand on Sunday, he can tell if you've been good or bad. I've sat with the prophet afterward, and he has told me which families good, and which families are are bad. He can tell if a person has a good spirit or a bad one. Be sure to look him in the eye, understand, though, that if you are guilty about anything, he will know.

"The devil is enraged, and he wants our young people. His work is that of anger," Uncle Jim declared with authority as Becca wrote every word with a purple pen.

> *"When you feel anger rise, you must fight it with sweetness. Anger itself is the devil at work. Smile, you must rise above the temptation to get angry. In fact, anything that would destroy a peaceful spirit must be resisted. We must stay sweet. Uncle Rulon warns us daily that the end will be soon. To be without peace is to be without protection from evil..."*

Becca listened carefully with the other children in her class as Uncle Jim, the family training teacher, described evil. For the most part, she was interested in the evil outside of the Crick and tried to remember the people she had known in Riverton who weren't part of their community. It didn't seem like many of them were evil. Maybe they were, and she just didn't know it.

Even so, it felt good to be at the Crick and be a part of the chosen people. Clearly, they were better than the outside world. Otherwise, why was the outside world going to come and attack them before the world came to an end?

She had heard many times from the Prophet, Uncle Rulon, that they were in the last days, and that "Outsiders" would come to take the food storage and supplies her people had saved. Proud to live at the Crick now, she pitied the apostates who lived outside of their beliefs. They would be destroyed.

Inevitably her thoughts went to her dad.

Was he evil? He was now an apostate, but *was he evil? Would he be destroyed?*

Questions circled her head like mosquitos, but she didn't dare ask. The last thing she wanted to do was burden her mother, so she decided the next time Grandma Claudia was around, she would try to get some answers.

That opportunity came the next day after school as they sat working a puzzle, and Becca jumped at the chance.

"Grandma, is Dad really an apostate?"

"Becca, what makes you think 'bout that?" Grandma looked up with a soft face.

"Uncle Jim said that anger is the work of the devil, and Uncle Rulon says everyone outside the Crick is goin' to come and take our food storage in the last days, so I wondered if Dad was one of those evil ones now?" Becca asked.

"That's for the Prophet to decide. I love having you here living with me. You are my little girl. Here, have another cookie," Grandmother Claudia handed her a cookie with a smile.

"What did you do at school today?" She asked, changing the subject.

Becca sighed, slumped in her chair and pushed away from the table. "It was boring. We read and did math problems. Why do we even have to go to school if it's so annoying?" She said, not really asking a question or wanting an answer.

She couldn't even begin to explain about Mr. Ferber, whose loud voice was scary. Besides, she missed her cousin, Desiree, who had been with her at school every day since Kindergarten.

"Let's try to think about somethin' happy," she reminded, "like babies and sunshine."

Becca thought about that and pictured Mr. Ferber in baby clothes.

"There, I see a smile already," Grandma encouraged.

Her grandma would not approve of what made her smile, so she kept that part a secret.

"How 'bout we get some work done while we're at it," Mother said sweetly as she entered the kitchen. Even though her mother tried to act like everything was fine, Becca knew she was stressed about money. She had gotten a job sewing watch bands, soda thermoses, and lanyards from home. The older children could earn a penny a piece for trimming threads after the items were sewn. Becca loved helping her mother, and loved making money too, so she grabbed some trimmers and eagerly got to work. Piling the trimmed pieces, Becca began to count. "1...2...3..."

Sometimes she felt as if there could be no better place on earth than right there in Grandpa John's house talking and working with Mother and Grandma Claudia. Everything was peaceful and happy, and if it weren't for lessons from Monday's family training classes, and warnings on Sunday from Uncle Rulon, the Prophet, she would never suspect bad things even went on in the world.

***

Saturdays were work-project days. The older boys and fathers would go to the church to be assigned community work. They would build houses, fix roofs, dig ditches, and help with farming or anything else that would come up. Ted and Benjamin had to get up early and leave with Grandpa John.

Sometimes mothers would go to the church and cook huge meals using the industrial-sized bread machines and ovens to feed all the workers. When that happened, the older girls would have to pick up the slack at home and take care of toddlers along with their other weekend chores. Becca didn't mind tending babies, but building a house seemed like a lot more fun, and she wished she could go build instead. But, to do that, she would have to work too closely with the boys, and that was not acceptable.

Sundays were strictly for church and family. Although getting ready was chaotic and church meetings could be dull, Becca loved huge Sunday dinners. Having two grandmothers in one house had some splendid benefits, and yummy meals were one of them, especially when desserts were involved. Carrot pudding was one of her favorite desserts, and her Grandma Claudia made it often. Grandma Leah, however, specialized in coffee cakes, which drew in uncles like ants to a picnic.

One Sunday after dinner, Dad showed up for an unexpected visit. Becca couldn't help but be excited. He always brought neat things, like toys or treats. He waited outside the fence, and Grandpa John went to speak with him.

"Children, come see me for a minute," Mother encouraged them to her room as their dad waited.

Once seated side-by-side on her bed, they listened solemnly.

"Today is Sunday, and if you go, you'll miss family prayer." She paused and looked at each one of them seriously, then continued, "Think about what the Prophet might want you to do." With that, she left them to think.

It *was* Sunday.

Dad *didn't* hold the priesthood.

They all knew what the Prophet would *want* them to do.

"I'm not going, and you guys shouldn't either," Tilly advised.

One by one, each child stood up from the bed and made their choice. Becca held on until the last moment with Janessa by her side. Both girls wanted to go with him, but the heaviness of the stares and expectations were too much. Janessa looked up, waiting to see what Becca would do.

"We'd better stay," Becca mumbled with disappointment. Shoulders down, Becca and Janessa left the room together. They went to the living room to look out the window to see their dad one last time before Mother would tell him they weren't coming. From the window, Becca could vaguely hear the exchange.

"Mary, I know they want to see me. I drove four hours to see my kids; you need to let me see them."

Pressing her palm to her cheek, she said, "Travis, they don't want to go. I gave 'em all a chance to decide for themselves."

Peeking through the front window, Becca waved as her dad turned to walk away from the fence. His brows were down-turned, but when he saw Becca, he smiled his big dad-smile and waved back. Ashamed she had been watching, and ashamed for pushing him away, Becca quickly yanked the curtain closed, ran into her room, and jumped onto her bed. She wished more than anything to understand why the Prophet declared him unworthy of the priesthood and felt terrible he couldn't even come inside.

Through the window, an orange, pink and blue sky reminded her of the first day they came to live at the Crick with Grandpa. It beckoned her to believe that some things were still the same. But it lied. Everything was different.

***

"Ted, Tilly, Benjamin, Justin, Janessa! Look what Dad brought!"

Kneeling on the couch, face pressed to the window, Becca yelled from behind Grandma's curtains. Eagar to see, the other children joined her.

"Oh cool!"

"Wow!"

"What is that?"

"It's a four-wheeler!" Ted yelled.

"All of you, come away from the window," Mother cautioned.

She stepped outside to speak with Travis, but before reaching his truck, the children rushed around her to check out their new toy.

With triumph, Travis put his hand on Ted's shoulder and announced, "Wanna go for a ride?"

"I don't know, Travis, he's awfully young," Mother resisted.

"Mary, I'll be with them and teach them how. They won't drive by themselves yet. And besides, I brought helmets. They'll be safe," Travis reasoned, putting his hands on his hips.

After a moment, Mother said, "Just one ride for Ted and Benjamin. I need to take them to Saturday work day."

"Mother, please let us stay. We wanna play with our new four-wheeler. We never miss. Just this once?" The boys begged.

Wanting the children to stay happy, Mother couldn't help but cave. "Ok, I guess just this once."

Excited squeals filled the air, piercing the mountainside. Becca watched her dad, and his face reminded her of Christmas morning. She hadn't seen him that happy in a long time, and it felt good.

Gesturing towards the truck, he said, "Hop in. We'll go down to the crick bed."

"Will you come with us, Mother?" Tilly asked.

Still reeling from the whole idea, Mother wrung her hands and said with a half-smile, "Well, not today. Travis, please be careful and make sure they wear a helmet."

"We'll be fine," Travis assured. "I won't let anything hurt my children."

"Ya, Mother, Dad'll take care of us," Becca reassured.

"We'll help watch Justin and Janessa," Tilly offered.

"I get the first ride because I'm the oldest," Ted asserted.

"Youngest to oldest, children," Mother said with her hands joined tightly, still unsure of the whole idea.

***

One by one the children put on a helmet and went for a ride, careful to wrap their hands tightly around their Dad's waist.

Becca's turn was right in the middle. It was a little tricky at first to get on without her dress flying up, but she quickly figured out how to tuck it under her legs. Glad to have the added cover of her leggings, Becca adjusted the best she could and then just had fun.

"You ready?" Dad asked.

"Yep!" She yelped and waved to her siblings who were all lined up on the wooden trailer that had carried the 4-wheeler.

While they were close to the trailer, Dad drove slowly, but as they approached the creek bed by the wash, he sped up. They blew past a family parked by the crick bed, and Becca loved the looks on the children's faces as she waved. Other people at the Crick had four-wheelers, but Becca felt like a celebrity. If Dad hadn't lost his priesthood, he would have been the coolest dad in town.

Rides went on all day until the sun was almost down. Except for snacking and bathroom breaks behind bushes, the children stayed on the wooden trailer and waited for their turn for a ride.

Dirt coated them, head to toe. Becca's hair looked like it was blond from the thick layer of dust. Even her teeth felt gritty, and she looked at Benjamin to see his teeth were lined with dirt like he had eaten it for dinner.

Just minutes later, dad announced, "It's getting late, we need to pack it up."

Resistant moans rose from the cruddy crew.

"We had a good time. I'll bring it again," he reassured.

He started to park the four-wheeler up onto the trailer, but instead turned to Ted and asked, "You wanna drive it to Grandpa John's and meet us there?"

"Why does Ted get to ride it back?" Becca said, disappointed.

Tilly started to speak but held back and made a pinched face with scrunched eyes.

"He's had a little more practice than everyone else," Travis reasoned.

"And I'm the oldest. And I'm a man," Ted reminded, making muscles. The girls moaned some more but knew it was done and, with little resistance, piled into the truck to drive back to Grandpa John's.

Ted parked the four-wheeler outside Grandpa's fence and hopped off just as they arrived.

The kids waved their goodbyes and went into the house to bathe. Becca noticed dad reached into his truck, grabbed a towel, drenched it with their drinking water, and wiped his face. He probably needed to come inside to use the restroom and freshen up, but Becca knew Mother wouldn't allow him in because he didn't hold the priesthood. Permitting such an act would destroy the dedication of their home.

Just as he was putting the towel back into his truck, she heard the familiar noise of a revving engine. "Someone's driving our four-wheeler!" Justin said.

At once they all charged out of the house. Tilly was driving the four-wheeler all by herself!

"Tilly, you get back here," Mother said sweetly, but her face looked anything but sweet. Becca thought Tilly had gone inside, but she must have gone back out without anyone noticing.

Dad hollered, "Tilly!"

All the children jumped at his voice. They were not used to that sort of yelling. Tilly pressed the gas harder, and the engine revved louder and louder as she tore off around the corner.

"Change gears! Change gears!" Dad yelled as he ran after her.

Tilly looked back at her dad and unintentionally ran off the road into a ditch.

"Tilly, Tilly, are you ok?" Dad said with both compassion and anger as he ran to her.

She emerged with a sober look on her face. "I'm ok. Just had a little wreck."

"You did not have permission to go ride by yourself!" Dad was thoroughly angry. He checked her out, and then looked at the brand-new four-wheeler which was scratched and dented.

"Tilly, you could have hurt yourself badly! And do you know how expensive that machine is? You have to respect things. You can't just go tearing them up. You probably stripped the gears." Every sentence he said got louder and angrier. The other children just stood back and watched. He was furious. Becca remembered Uncle Jim's talk about anger. He had said, *"The devil is enraged... His work is that of anger."*

"You don't get to tell me what to do," Tilly replied, pushed him away, and ran into the house.

Mother was the first to speak. "Travis, it was an accident," she said calmly. It was her way of reminding him to keep his anger in check without sounding bossy or disrespectful in front of the children.

"Mary. Any dad would be angry. She could have gotten hurt. And she needs to learn to respect things. They cost money. Money doesn't just grow on trees."

He backed the four-wheeler out of the ditch and drove it onto the trailer.

"The gears seem to be ok," he said and looked up at the children.

"Next time I come, I'll teach you all how to drive. No one gets to ride unless I say so from now on," he said more patiently.

The children gave him hugs and said goodbye. It was getting dark, and he had a 4-hour drive to get back to Riverton.

That night after she washed the dirt of the day away, Becca tried to make sense of the last exchange between Mother and Dad. He had said, *any dad would be angry.* What did that mean? Any normal dad who held the priesthood would have kept sweet. He was wrong. Uncle Jim said that anger was the work of the devil.

No wonder the Prophet declared dad an apostate. He doesn't even know what's normal.

4

CAMPING AND A REAL JOB
1994

"Becca, whatcha doin'?" Mother asked from behind her video camera.

"Settin' up our tent," Becca said as she unfolded the tent to smooth it out. Without looking up, she fiddled with the parts and organized the pieces according to their placement.

"I think Uncle Seth is going to have to help," Mother offered.

Pushing fly-away hairs from her face, Becca beamed back, "I think I can figure it out."

Next to blading or riding bikes, camping was her favorite thing to do. She fed the poles into the canvas tent and forced it upright. A tent pole was missing, and it wasn't perfect, but she was determined to complete her mission. Her sister, Tilly, and her cousin, Joanna, set up their tiny, two-people-tent a few feet away from where Becca worked.

Mother walked over to film the girls' progress and said, "You girls can help Becca set up ours when you're done."

"Ok, Mother," Tilly said, and turned shyly from the camera.

As her mother walked around filming and narrating the happenings at camp, Becca worked on doing it without assistance from the older girls. Not that she didn't like help, she did. But for some reason when her sister got involved, it turned into a bossy fest in which somehow Tilly ended up "right," Becca got in trouble for being angry, and nothing really got done.

After one last attempt, Becca announced, "It's missin' a pole. Uncle Seth will just have to do it."

"Mother told you that," Tilly reminded.

"I know, but I just wanted to try and figure it out if I could," Becca countered with a big smile leaving Tilly no resistance to argue back.

Adjusting her dress that covered her jeans and longies, Becca stood and decided to explore the mountains she loved. To her left, she could see Grandma Claudia sitting in a folding chair next to Uncle Seth's truck reading comics from the Sunday paper with Justin peering over her shoulder. Janessa was beside them jumping over a rock. Her blonde, braided hair was scraggly and looked like a mess atop her cute pink dress. Ahead, Becca could see a thick forest of white-barked Aspens. To her right, she saw Uncle Seth, Ted, and Benjamin setting up their tents.

"Uncle Seth, our tent is missin' a pole, so I can't set it up. Will you fix it for us?" She asked.

"I found an extra pole in my bag. It's probably yours. We'll get to it right after this," he said.

"Thank you," she beamed and took off to the trees.

Uncle Seth was the best uncle. He lived with them at Grandpa John's house. It was good to have him with them. In fact, if he hadn't come, they wouldn't have been able to go at all. Mother never would have taken them camping without the covering of the priesthood, which Uncle Seth provided.

There was something about the freedom of the breeze, the open campfire, and the vast night sky that always spoke to Becca. Remembering stories of the great pioneers who traveled by foot with oxen and covered wagons to settle at the Crick, she wondered how it was to live off the land and cook over fires full time. For some reason, that always sounded like it would be fun.

She was perfectly happy to just be in the woods with a tent and her pillows and warm blankets. The only thing that could make it more perfect would be if dad, the old dad who held the priesthood, were there with the four-wheeler, and if Desiree was there to ride it with her.

Even so, Becca was beginning to have serious doubts about her dad. He *had* done something to lose the priesthood, and she knew the prophet *had* separated them from him for a good reason. An apostate now, even to the point that he showed anger openly; he couldn't be entirely trusted.

Eager to explore, Becca moved deeper into the forest to see if she could find something interesting, like pretty rocks or wildflowers. White Aspens surrounded her, and she stepped carefully, looking for signs of animals. She noticed moss on some rocks and then, just in the distance, there was some movement. It was a buck with its head held high.

As tall as Uncle Seth, it dwarfed Becca and walked like it knew something she didn't. Gently, it turned its big antlered head and gazed toward their camp. Barely breathing, eyes glued to the deer, Becca tried to inch her way closer and then stopped, not 10 paces away.

Starting to feel dizzy and lightheaded, she realized she had been holding her breath. Becca exhaled, and two round, black eyes turned to meet her stare. She had never been this close to a deer before and noticed it even had eyelashes. Looking into its eyes, she decided the majestic creature was beautiful.

"Deer!"

Rowdy with excitement, Ted and Benjamin joined her.

As suddenly as it had appeared, the buck scurried off into the thick forest.

Frustrated by their presence, Becca said, "Go find your own buck."

"We can find one together," Benjamin offered.

Realizing she sounded mean, Becca said, "That's ok, I'm sure any deer around here is probably long gone now."

"Sorry we scared him away," Benjamin said.

"Not me, he could've poked you with his horns and then chewed off your leg. Those things can be mean, especially to a girl," Ted teased.

"It didn't look mean to me. It had eyelashes longer than mine," Becca defended.

No one could get under her skin as much as Ted. He knew how to work a person. He'd find a way to push until there were tears or screams. Either way, she wasn't going to play his game, so she stopped in front of a tree, pulled out her knife, and began to carve.

"Whatcha gonna carve?" Benjamin asked.

Putting his mouth about an inch from her ear, Ted sneered in a high-pitched voice, "Probably something girly with eyelashes."

"I don't know, stick around and see," Becca countered with a smile as if his invasion of her space mattered nothing at all.

It was an invite for them to stay and it worked. Not two minutes later, both Ted and Benjamin were off carving trees of their own. At least Becca could have space to breathe.

Triumph. Becca had stopped the rising anger before it could take root. She knew how evil a temper was and how children were to keep a quiet spirit. Becca felt a little guilty for getting angry about the buck. It just didn't seem right that Ted should get away with being so mean, while she had to work so hard not to get angry.

Vowing to be better, Becca knew what to carve. Carefully she notched out the letters, K.E.E.P...S.W.E.E.T. There. Uncle Rulon would be proud.

Satisfied with her handy work, Becca looked up just as Mother rushed over with the video camera. Tilly and Joanna were close behind.

"I heard someone yell deer. Where is it?"

"Ted and Benjamin scared it away," Becca sighed and kept carving.

"What does it say, Becca?" Mother asked, focusing in on the tree.

Lifting the knife to point out the message, Becca read carefully, "Keep Sweet."

"'Keep Sweet, awe, that's nice," Mother hummed and moved on with the camera to see what the other children were carving. By that time everyone, even Tilly and Joanna, had carved their initials. Stepping back eyeing her work, Becca straightened her dress, tucked her flyaway hairs behind her ears, and lifted her chin.

Catching on to the fun of being filmed, Ted started to make monkey noises and pretended to hang from the trees, and the other children followed suit.

Becca left the silliness to stand by the river and see if she could spot some crawdads. Picking up a stick, she calmly poked it into the water. Claws came out of the murky water and clamped down. Crawdads were so easy to predict. A person didn't even have to bait a hook. Their claws would grab whatever was put in the water and hold on for dear life. If a person didn't have any food, they could just catch a crawdad, cook it over a fire, and eat it like a little lobster. Becca felt sorry for the dumb creatures who didn't think to protect themselves. They just did what the other crawdads did without any thought, and then got eaten for dinner. In a way, it was sad.

It didn't take long for all the other children to join her by the water.

"Whatcha got there?" Mother asked, and then everyone turned toward Becca.

"Crawdads," Becca explained, lifting one out of the water with her stick. Tilly and Joanna squealed, and the boys laughed and went to grab their own sticks.

"Should we catch some and eat 'em for dinner?" Ted asked.

"Oh, I don't know, we brought a lot of food," Mother answered.

"What do they taste like?" Becca asked.

"Probably like fried Chicken," Ted answered, and they all laughed.

Laying the camera down, Mother said, "Go ahead and put him back. We don't have a bucket. Maybe next time. Let's get back to camp and help Grandma Claudia with dinner."

***

After a chilly night's sleep, Becca awoke to the sound of Uncle Seth building a fire to heat water for hot chocolate and cook breakfast. Even though she was cold, Becca couldn't think of staying in her cozy sleeping bag. Not wanting to miss a thing, she unzipped the tent and climbed out.

"Good-mornin', Becca," Mother said sweetly.

"Mornin', Bec," followed Uncle Seth.

"Good mornin'," Becca, hummed as she grabbed a marshmallow out of a bag to roast for a pre-breakfast snack.

Smoke from the fire irritated her eyes as she put the white, squishy bit on the end of a stick and poked it into the red coals. Benjamin, Janessa, and Justin wandered up, sat next to the warm fire, and stared like they were still half asleep. After a few minutes, Justin stood up and chased flying ashes. Giggling at her goofy little brother, Becca took the now honey colored snack off the edge of her stick, blew on it, and placed the whole thing in her mouth.

"Hey now, that's a big bite for such a little lady," Uncle Seth teased.

Becca smiled and fought to keep the gooeyness in her mouth.

Uncle Seth was so cool. He was a chef at The Golden Circle, a restaurant in Hurricane that Grandpa John owned. Grateful for his presence and his sense of humor, Becca swallowed the marshmallow and asked, "Uncle Seth, is it fun workin' at the restaurant?"

"Most of the time, yes. But it is an awful lot of work."

"You get to eat a lot?"

"Well mostly I work, but I do eat too."

"You ever feed mean people?"

"Most people are friendly, but we can get some complainers."

"Uncle Rulon says apostates are dangerous and want to come and divide us and take our food storage. Do you ever get scared of 'em?"

"Nah. Most people seem to be pretty happy after they get their food," he reassured.

Becca thought about it. Fed people *were* happy people.

"Besides," Uncle Seth added, "it's good for the Gentiles to see how good we are, too."

"I could help at your restaurant if you ever have too much work," she said in-between licking sticky fingers. "I'd help lots, and maybe you can teach me how to cook."

Uncle Seth looked genuinely interested. "Mary, you think Becca could come help me sometimes at the Golden Circle? We could sure use a dishwasher."

Immediately Becca's heart began to race. She hadn't thought he would consider it. It just seemed like fun. Seeing Becca's flushed face, Mother reluctantly replied.

"Oh, I don't know Seth, do you think it would be ok for a young girl?"

"Mother, I'd be ok with Uncle Seth," Becca added.

"Well, we could try it a few times. She could ride down with Levi and me…"

Interrupting Uncle Seth, Becca exclaimed, "And, I love to do dishes!"

"Stacy Barlow, Simon's girl, just started and she could help Becca learn the kitchen," Uncle Seth said.

"Oh, Stacy! I love Stacy," Becca interrupted, again. She had only met her a few other times at a community gathering with some of her aunts but had enjoyed her humor.

"Would you like that Becca?" Mother asked.

"Oh, heck yeah! Yes, I would!" She said, thrilled by the idea.

"Watch your words," Mother reminded.

"We leave at 4:30 in the mornin' on Saturdays. You think you could be up by then?" Uncle Seth questioned with a professional look on his face.

"Oh, heck yes, I can!" Becca answered, ignoring Mother's look.

"Can you say anything other than 'Oh, heck yes'?" Becca heard from Ted's tent.

"Oh, heck yes!" Becca yelled even louder towards Ted.

Shaking her head, Mother said, "Oh, my stars. You children, I don't know what I'm gonna do with you!"

Ignoring Ted's teasing and Mother's worry about Becca's strong choice of words, Uncle Seth said, "Well then, let's get some practice. You can help with the eggs."

***

Becca felt that if there were a breeze, she would just float away. It was pitch dark and colder than she thought it would be at 4:30 in the morning, but she didn't complain. She hopped into Uncle Seth's truck along with Levi, and they headed off to Hurricane. It was the first day of her first real job at the Golden Circle.

Uncle Seth advised Becca as he drove, "I was thinkin' you could help clear tables if the dishes aren't too heavy. I can show you how to run the dishwasher, and you'll need to put dishes away too."

He didn't know who he was talking to. Becca had no intention of letting dishes pile up or anything else under her watch.

"Stacy can help teach you where everythin' goes and how things work." Levi chimed in. Levi was one of her Uncle's best friends, so he was practically part of the family and Becca looked up to him.

"Ok," she answered.

Besides keeping busy, Becca was most excited about working with Stacy. It didn't matter that Becca was barely eleven and Stacy was old enough to be placed in marriage, she already felt as if they were equals. After all, there was a restaurant to run.

The Golden Circle was attached to a gas station in Hurricane. It was a small town without many restaurants, so it was popular. As the truck pulled up to the station, Becca noticed her stomach was a bit nervous from eating breakfast so early.

The sun was just beginning to rise, and the restaurant looked strangely empty without lights and customers. Uncle Seth took her into the back and gave her an apron that was two sizes too big while Levi turned on lights and unlocked the front door. Becca folded the apron in half and tied it on as best she could. She felt important being in the kitchen where customers couldn't go.

"Becca!" Stacy walked in with open arms and gave her a hug and asked, "You excited for your first day?"

Becca curtsied and smoothed her apron with a goofy grin. Stacy grabbed her own apron and pulled it over her blue dress, careful not to mess up her brown, carefully braided hair.

Stacy had just enough time to show Becca where the dish soap was and where to stack the washed dishes before customers arrived.

As quickly as the dirty dishes came in, Becca would wash, dry, and put them away. Too petite to put the dishes away on the top rack without assistance, she pushed a chair over to the counter and stepped onto it to reach the shelf.

Occasionally, Stacy would come back to check on Becca and give her a thumb's up, but Becca could tell she was a little stressed.

Eager to help outside of the kitchen, Becca poked her head out the service window next to her Uncle where he delivered the finished pates to be served, and ask Uncle Seth, "You think Stacy needs some help out there?"

"I think she could use some help clearin' dishes. See what you can do," he encouraged with a wink. "Be sure to stay out of her way if she's rushin'. We want to make a good impression on our customers," he encouraged.

Lifting the apron over her head, Becca eagerly stepped out into the dining area to see what she could do.

At first glance, she only looked at the tables and dishes. Once she was closer, she started to notice the people. Women wore shorts and thin strapped shirts, and some of the men wore shorts and T-shirts with flip-flops. She had seen how apostates dressed in Utah, but that had been a while, and she wasn't used to it. It was almost embarrassing to be close to that much skin.

"Excuse me, young lady, can I get some more juice?" A lady with skin the color of Grandpa's creamed coffee held up her glass.

She had never seen anyone up close with that color skin, let alone talk to them.

Becca looked up to find Stacy smiling with a nod to suggest she should help the customer.

"Sure," she grinned.

She scurried off to grab the pitcher from the refrigerator, returned in a flash, and poured it into the small glass with a shaky hand.

The customer must have noticed she was a little nervous and patted her on her hand. "You're doing great."

"Thank you."

Smiling, Becca took some empty plates, then promptly returned to the kitchen to wash another batch of dishes. Each time she left the sink and walked out into the dining area, she felt more confident and less awkward.

For lunch, Uncle Seth made her the restaurant's special sandwich, a Monte Cristo. It was a warm French toast sandwich with two kinds of meat, house sauce, gooey cheese and a side of blueberry yogurt to dip it in. Becca couldn't help but feel fancy, except she had to gobble it and get back to the dishes.

Time flew, and it seemed like a blink when Uncle Seth met her in the kitchen and said, "We're done for the day. It's time to head back home."

"Uncle Seth, what do you think?" Becca asked as they drove home late that evening.

"Think about what?" Uncle Seth answered.

"'Bout me working at the Golden Circle. Did I do good? Can I come back?"

"Well, that's up to your mother, but I have to say you and Stacy make a good team," he admitted.

"Thanks, Uncle Seth! You'll see, I'll be the hardest worker ever."

"Oh, heck yes," He added with a wink.

***

"Order up!"

Becca walked to the service window, hopped up and propped herself on the ledge as she grabbed the two plates, and shimmied down and walked over to deliver two sandwiches.

Clapping softly, the two regular customers beamed, "We love it when you do that!"

Not even aware she had done anything out of the ordinary, Becca tucked a loose hair behind her ear, straightened her shoulders, and smiled, "Can I get you anythin' else?"

"Isn't she so cute?" The older man said, eyes twinkling under two gray eyebrows. "You are such a young professional girl. How old are you?"

Honored to be called professional, Becca proudly answered, "I'm twelve."

"Twelve going on twenty!" He teased.

Becca had served the older couple the week before and they had left her a big tip, so she instantly liked them.

"Where did you get your dress? I'd love to buy one for my granddaughter," asked the older woman. "She loves those *Little House on the Prairie* books, and I think she'd love to have a dress like that."

"My Mother makes my clothes. They're not really for sale." Becca answered.

"Order up!" Uncle Seth dinged the bell from the serving window.

"I'll get it," Becca said, then walked to the window, hopped up, and propped herself on the ledge. As she grabbed a plate with a fat, juicy hamburger and fries, Stacy asked her, "Everything alright, Becca Sue Louie Blue?"

"Yeah, they just wanted to know about my dress and asked how old I was."

"You want me to take over?" Stacy offered.

"Nah, I got it," Becca said.

"Well, if they ask too many questions, let me know, and I'll come help," Stacy assured.

Becca smiled reassuringly and nodded. Since starting the Golden Circle, she and Stacy had grown close. Mother had even let her spend the night several times. Her friendship helped Becca adjust to not having Desiree, and she was very grateful for it. She couldn't figure out why Stacy would be so concerned with the old couple asking questions, though. They weren't mean. In fact, they seemed quite nice for being Gentiles.

Still confused over Stacy's concern, Becca took the burger to a young man sitting by himself at the corner booth.

"Becca, I need you to work on dishes, now," Uncle Seth said, as he walked out from the kitchen, drying his hands on a clean towel.

Uncle Seth rarely told her to do anything. She knew what needed to be done without someone telling her, but the uneasy expression on his face made her do what he said without question.

Peeking through the door, Becca watched as Uncle Seth sat in the booth next to the young man. He seemed familiar, but Becca couldn't place him. Uncle Seth put his hand gently on the man's shoulder and then she recognized him. It was Sam, her cousin from her Mom's side. If he hadn't been wearing shorts and a t-shirt, she would have known him right off. Those clothes could mean only one thing. He was an apostate.

Guilt flooded in, so she closed the door and got busy doing dishes. It was one thing to serve Gentiles lunch and dinner, but it was another thing altogether to serve or help in any way someone who had left the Crick.

At once, she wondered what the prophet would say. Her dad was the only apostate she knew who wasn't at the Crick, but that was different because he was working to get back his priesthood. Sam was at least 10 years older than Becca, but she remembered him from family gatherings. He hadn't seemed like a bad person then.

"Stacy, why is Uncle Seth sitting with Sam? What did he do to become an apostate?"

"Well, we just need to be careful and trust that the Prophet set him apart for a good reason. You don't need to worry about it, though. Just stay busy."

"Ok, I guess." Unsatisfied, Becca swirled the dishrag in the air and turned to put away the dishes.

"How about you ride home with me, tonight?" Stacy offered as if she knew Becca was feeling left out.

"I'd love that!" Becca was instantly game.

"We can ask Uncle Seth. I think he'll be ok with it."

"Yay!" Freshly motivated, Becca scurried to get her work done.

Uncle Seth agreed Becca could ride home with Stacy, and the two girls jumped into her car. Becca sat tall in the front passenger seat and resisted the urge to open the glove box in front of her. She never got to sit in the front and had never been in a little car. The only vehicle their family used was a van. Stacy tuned the radio to country music, and the girls listened happily as they drove back to the Crick.

Becca knew her mother would not approve of the beat and words of the songs, but she felt safe. Stacy was so much fun and besides, Uncle Seth, who held the priesthood, had approved. That was all she needed.

5

A NEW NAME AND THE GRAND CANYON

1995

"Children, children, come in and sit down; I have some exciting news." Mother rushed them into the house with a big grin one day after school.

Hyped from their Mother's excitement, the children filed into Grandpa John's living room and took a space on the couch to receive the news.

"We're gonna get a new family. Grandfather called and told me that the Prophet has said I am to be married to a new man who holds the priesthood. Make some guesses who."

"Ted Williams."

"Alex Steed."

"Uncle Warren."

Names flew around the room like a game show. Feeding off their Mother's excitement, the children bounced on the couch throwing out guesses.

"No, but I'll give you a hint, one of my sisters is already married to him," Mother offered and then clasped her hands and raised her shoulders.

With that bit of information, all chaos broke loose. Cousins! They would be living with cousins! Instead of guessing about a new father, they all started thinking about their new siblings. Living with cousins would be like having a sleepover every night with best friends.

Seeing that the guessing game was getting them nowhere, Mother finally caved. "I'm marrying Uncle Arlen."

Squeals of delight filled Grandpa John's house as the children danced around and shot out comments like popcorn.

"Mother will be his third wife."

"Uncle Arlen will be our new father!"

"Our new name will be Johnson."

"Aunt Claudia will be our other mother!"

"Who's the other Mother?"

"Susan." Mother reminded.

"Mother Susan will be our other mother!"

Whoops filled the room and they continued to dance around.

Proud of their new status change, the children couldn't help but celebrate the Prophet's decision to place their mother with Uncle Arlen. He lived on the Arizona side of the Crick which was the "more modern" side of town.

Excited to be cool, Becca said, "Wait. Will we go to the Arizona school?"

"No, Becca, we'll still live with Grandpa John for a bit, and Father Arlen will join us every third evening."

Disappointed, Becca sighed.

"Sometimes, we'll have your new brothers and sisters over to sleep, and we'll have big family events where we all stay together, like camping. Father has plans to add to their big house for our whole family. All mothers and children will live together then, but that won't be for a while."

A new Father with three mothers, cousins to be brothers and sisters, and a new house on the Arizona side was as exciting as Christmas mornings back in Utah. Eager for the change, the whole next day, Becca could hardly think of anything else. She went to sleep thinking and dreaming about it, and then woke up the same way. Mother would be a third wife. They would be a part of a big family just like everyone else. Uncle Arlen was married to Becca's favorite aunt. Becca couldn't wait to see Desiree and Stacy and tell them the news.

A few nights later, Mother left for a couple of hours and then returned home with their new Father. He said the family prayer and blessed the children. He was a little bigger than what Becca remembered but still wore the same kind smile.

"You're all Johnsons now," he announced.

Glowing from head to toe, Mother clapped her hands quietly and smiled as the children cheered with excitement.

"Let's go to the ice-cream parlor to celebrate," Father suggested.

Excited to share their family's news, the children quickly got ready and made their way to the van. It was the first time they would be in public as a 3-mother family with a Father who held the priesthood. By the way news spread, everyone at the Crick would know there were six new Johnson's in town before church on Sunday.

"Stacy!" Becca recognized her car as they drove up to the parlor. She couldn't wait to share the news.

"Becca, wait for Father to stop the van," mother cautioned as they parked.

Wanting to make a good impression on Father, Becca lowered her voice and said, "I will, I just can't wait to tell her."

All the children filed into the parlor. Stacy was standing at the door, so Becca quickly shared the news.

"Mother married Uncle Arlen, and now we're all Johnsons."

"That's exciting, I'm so happy for you!" Stacy said and hugged her tight.

"I have to get home. Four o'clock comes early," Stacy said looking at the clock.

With all the excitement, Becca had forgotten about the Golden Circle.

"You should come stay the night at my house and ride to work with me," Stacy offered.

Becca looked at her mother who then turned to Father.

"We'll see, I'll have to talk it over with your Mother," Father said.

Stacy smiled and waved goodbye as Becca's family walked up to order. A little disappointed, Becca had to think about what had just happened. She was used to asking her Mother to do things. Father Arlen's permission was not something she had considered.

***

It wasn't until the next school day when Becca proudly wrote her new name as a Johnson, that something occurred to her. Maybe Dad wouldn't be as excited as they were. It felt a little like she was shoving him off to the side when she didn't write Darger down. But, he still didn't hold the priesthood, and now they were a part of a family with a father who did. They were the ones doing the right thing. Travis would just have to understand.

Beaming from ear to ear, Becca practiced writing her new name with different colored pens. Johnson was longer than Darger and sounded way better. Walking through the halls at school, she couldn't help but feel a little bit taller than the day before.

That afternoon, just around dinner time, Travis showed up at Grandpa John's fence. Father went outside to greet him, and Grandma Claudia gently gathered the children, encouraging them to the other side of the house to help with chores before dinner, speaking nothing of their dad's arrival.

"Travis won't be visiting today," Mother announced as she entered the dining room where the children were setting the table.

Once dinner was prepared and the table filled with food, Father came in and asked the meal to be blessed. He then announced, "This weekend I'm taking our whole family on a camping trip."

Excited squeals erupted from the dinner table. The children didn't even have time to think about what had just happened with Travis. Becca, however, couldn't help but feel like they were hurting his feelings.

She also realized she had to work on Saturday.

"But I have work," she reminded.

"You'll just have to miss this time. Uncle Seth will make do," Mother assured.

As much as she loved the Golden Circle, she enjoyed camping more and was excited to share it with her new brothers and sisters. It had been a while since she had been on a big family vacation. And, this was going to be the biggest, yet.

***

The next day was all abuzz with everyone getting things together. It was Thursday, and they were going to miss two days of school, so everyone was in a happy mood. The older children helped the younger ones pack as Mother readied food and supplies. Father went to his big house for the day to get the rest of the family, so it was all up to them to get ready at Grandpa John's.

Around noon four vans, the last one pulling a large box trailer with enough stuff to fill a house, showed up outside Grandpa John's. All Becca knew was that they were going to camp somewhere by the Grand Canyon. Cousins, who were now her brothers and sisters poured out of the vehicles and helped them load their bags into the trailer.

Jerusha, Mother Susan's daughter who was around Becca's age, came up and hugged Becca, and they decided to sit by each other on the drive. One by one, the newly acclaimed brothers and sisters found traveling buddies for the trip. Father said a prayer to bless their travels, and the four vehicles pulled out of Grandpa John's, caravanning towards the Grand Canyon.

There were so many stories to share with her new sisters, that it seemed as if no time had passed at all when the vans stopped at the camping site.

As if rehearsed a hundred times before, the older children started setting up tents and helped watch the younger children while the Mothers set up the food area. Father and the older boys unloaded the bulky items and unloaded the trailer. Becca and Jerusha wasted no time and had their tent up first. As she looked around at the busyness, Becca couldn't help but feel proud. This was her family.

Hoping to have some fun with Jerusha before dinner, Becca asked, "Wanna go explore?" Eager to please, Jerusha agreed, "Sure."

Tall pine trees surrounded the camping area, but just a little way off, the trees disappeared, and rocky canyon walls similar to the canyon walls at the Crick surrounded them. The blue sky contrasted by the orange-brown of the earth made color seem alive as the two hiked the rocky terrain. Their hike had to be a short one. It was early evening, and the Mothers would have dinner ready soon. In the shadows cast by the higher rocks it was already getting chilly, but it felt good.

Breathing in the crisp air, Becca asked, "Couldn't you just live here?"

"Oh, I don't know. I like it and all, but it isn't home," Jerusha answered.

"But wouldn't it be fun to cook on a fire and sleep under the stars every night? We could pick up all the shimmery rocks and keep a collection because we'd keep them here, and we could hike whenever we wanted." Becca said.

Considering the idea, Jerusha asked, "What about the church, and the Prophet? What if the destructions happened and we weren't at the Crick?"

She had a point. It would be unfortunate if they weren't at the Crick during those days. Every Cricker knew that when the destructions came, only the righteous FLDS chosen people would be lifted up while all the land would be wiped clean. Once purified, the chosen people would be set back down to start the new world.

Down the path from where they had hiked, a familiar voice called, "Becca! Jerusha! Girls!"

It was Tilly walking with Wendy, Mother Susan's daughter.

With all the authority of a big sister, Tilly exclaimed, "Mother needs you to help with the younger children while we get dinner ready."

Reluctantly, Becca turned, and the four girls marched the short way back to camp. On their way, they passed several of the brothers trekking about like they didn't have a care in the world.

***

Around the campfire, before they went into their tents for the night, Father read from scripture and offered evening prayer. Then, he announced he was going to take the older children, both boys and girls on a hike down into the Grand Canyon the next day.

"Everyone, make sure to have water and some snacks. We'll head out early before the sun rises. It gets pretty hot in the afternoon," he said.

A real hike! Becca and the older kids were stoked. Becca and Jerusha filled their water bottles and grabbed some crackers and grapes. Becca liked to be prepared way ahead of time and imagined how busy it would be in the morning with all the other children scrambling to get ready. That just wasn't her way.

She wanted to ask Father how long it would be, but he had already turned in for the night to Mother Susan's tent. If it was her Mother's tent that would be one thing, but Mother Susan's was another. Becca didn't know her very well and felt awkward around her. Questions had to wait until morning.

The sky was still dark blue as sleepy, uncombed heads poked their ways out of tents. Becca was up first because she was used to getting up early on Saturdays. If this were the Crick, she would have already been up for an hour, on her way to work.

All of the Mothers were still asleep in their tents with the younger children, so the older kids had to get breakfast for themselves. Becca grabbed a few pieces of beef jerky and an apple while some of the boys, including Ted, thought they would be funny and downed a whole bag of marshmallows.

"Hey, Becca, don't you wish you could eat a delicious marshmallow?" Ted teased waving the bag in front of her face as if he was the smartest boy in town.

Ignoring his comment, Becca bit into her apple and turned the other direction towards her tent to get her zip-up jacket. It was cold now, but she knew it would be hot once the sun came up and would need something she could take off and tie around her waist.

By the time she found it under her sleeping bag, Father had gotten up and started gathering everyone together.

With a solemn look, he said, "We'll be hiking clear down into the canyon. Everyone pair up with a sister or brother, so that no one will be alone. We should be back to camp by noon, and the Mothers will have lunch ready for us."

He said a quick prayer and the light-hearted gang headed out.

The boys commandeered the front of the line ahead of Father, while the girls, Tilly, Wendy, Jerusha, and Becca maintained the caboose. The canyon gave everyone permission to be in good humor. Becca noticed Tilly even relaxed a bit.

Poor girl, she just needs to let loose and stop being the big sister once in a while.

Putting one arm around Jerusha and one arm around Tilly, Becca said, "Howdy, sisters."

Joining the trio, Wendy put her arm around Tilly, and the group of four giggled and walked blissfully arm in arm until forced apart by the narrowing path.

As the day wore on, Wendy and Tilly lagged farther and farther behind, slipping out of sight with the boys so far ahead on the trail, it was almost like Becca and Jerusha were all by themselves. It was chilly, and for once, Becca was glad to be wearing so many layers of clothing. In the heat of the summer, longies, leggings, jeans, and dress were unbearable. She hoped it would stay chilly, but she knew once the sun came up it would change.

"Do you ever wish you didn't have to wear your longies, leggings, and pants?" Becca asked Jerusha.

"Oh, Becca, why'd you think of that?" She fretted and put her hand on her heart. "I like my longies. They keep me safe."

It was taught that in the last days, evil men with swords would come to kill the righteous, but if believers were clothed in garments, they would be protected as weapons wouldn't go past the heavenly gear. Even though Becca knew this and was thankful to have the protection, she still wondered occasionally what it would be like to be free from so much bulk.

"They just get so hot, that's all," Becca said, feeling guilty.

As if the sun heard the complaint about her longies as an invite, it peered over the eastern horizon, instantly warming her face. Becca couldn't help but smile and took a long, intoxicating breath of the morning air.

The rocks of the canyon, too, seemed to take in a breath as they greeted the sun with colors only nature could display. Orange, brown, blue, and yellow rocks awoke from the sleepy gray they were just minutes before.

Along the path the girls enjoyed long moments of silence, then spurts of talking or singing church songs. Oblivious to time, they just enjoyed the hike. The path was laid out pretty well and, except for the rocky areas where they had to descend carefully with their dresses, so they wouldn't trip, it had been somewhat easy. However, Becca noticed the rocky terrain was increasing along with the heat of the sun, making the hike more and more challenging.

"Let's stop and have a snack," Becca said. Finding a shady spot on the side of a rock, they pulled out some crackers and grapes and sat to eat.

"What time is it?" Jerusha asked.

Pulling her watch out of her bag, Becca exclaimed, "Wow, it's almost nine!" They had been hiking for three and a half hours.

Just above them on the path, they could see Wendy and Tilly getting closer and closer.

"Let's surprise them!" Becca said.

"Ok," Jerusha snickered.

Both Tilly and Wendy had scowls on their faces. They didn't look happy at all as they approached.

"Boo!" Becca shouted as she jumped out from the shade-rock right in front of the older girls.

"Don't do that Becca! You know I don't like that!" Tilly snarled.

"Just having fun. Why're you so mad?" Becca said, defensively.

"Well, first I'm not angry. I just don't like being scared. Scaring people is mean. You need to consider that before you play like that!"

Becca noticed Wendy looking at her grapes.

"Want some? We packed a lot," she offered.

"Yes, please, we only brought one granola bar, and we ate it a while ago," Wendy said, a smile returning to her face.

"Can I have a drink, too?" Wendy asked.

"Where's your water?" Becca asked.

Tilly huffed off mumbling under her breath.

"Tilly thought we could just share one, so we didn't have to carry so much, and we already drank it all," Wendy said.

"Oh, that's not cool," Becca said, then handed Wendy the bottle. She had been careful to ration her water but had already consumed over half, and they still had to climb their way up.

Walking back towards the girls, Tilly said, "I think we should start back."

Thankfully, in the distance, they could see Father, Ted and Benjamin and a few other brothers heading up the canyon toward them. Relieved for their timing, the girls turned back toward camp.

Climbing the canyon was a whole different hike. Before Becca knew it, the sun was straight overhead, and all four girls had exhausted their water bottles. The boys, who had raced ahead hours before now lagged behind the girls. Tilly got even grouchier, and no one said a word.

Behind them, Becca could see Father talking to Ted who was sitting on a rock spitting something out of his mouth. She couldn't say for sure, but it looked like he was crying. For the first time in a long time, she felt a little sorry for Ted. Perhaps, marshmallows for breakfast was not the best idea.

Sweat poured down Becca's face, and she started to get dizzy. With everything in her, she resisted the urge to take off the layers of clothing that hung on her like blankets, holding in her body heat. For a minute she regretted sharing her water with Wendy and Tilly. But it was already done. Closing her mouth to keep it from getting dry in the scorching heat, she dragged one foot in front of the other.

The canyon that had offered such beauty just hours before became a dreadful chore. Becca checked her watch. It was almost eleven. Rumbling, her stomach announced its hunger and for a split second, she wished she hadn't given up her snacks.

Suddenly, Wendy and Tilly sat down and began to cry. Jerusha followed. Mustering all the courage she could, Becca tried to find the bright side. "We're almost done. Look, I remember that rock. It looks like a horse. We'll be out in a few minutes."

Three pairs of blank eyes stared at her as if she was crazy.

"When we get back, we can run our heads under water and then take a long nap. Mother Claudia brought those yummy cookies she makes, and we can eat some." Jerusha and Wendy looked at Tilly and started to perk up.

"Come on, let's get there before the boys," Becca encouraged.

Without a word, all three girls stood up and started walking again.

Thankfully, moments later, they could see where the trail started. They *were* going to make it. Moods lifted, and the pace quickened. Becca never thought the sound of playing children could make her feel so lighthearted as they dragged themselves into camp.

"Hi, girls." Becca's mother was the first of the mothers to greet them. "How was the hike?"

"It was fun, but I'm tired and starving," Becca answered as she and the other girls filled their water bottles.

"It got so hot," Jerusha said.

"And, we didn't have enough water," Wendy said.

"And, I think Ted may have thrown up," Becca added.

"Oh, my," Mother Claudia said and walked toward the boys who had started to file into camp, followed by Father.

Mother Susan stood with her hands on her hips without saying a word.

Dull from the hard hike, Becca took an apple, three cookies, and a full water bottle into her tent. Tears of tension fell as she laid down on her sleeping bag, happy to find rest. Fighting the urge to keep sweet, she allowed herself to feel proud for finishing the hike without throwing up or complaining like everyone else.

6

CALM BEFORE THE STORM
1996

As far back as Becca could remember it seemed like the house had a baby in it. She missed tiny hands and the smell of pink baby lotion. Even though there were plenty of cousins and friends with little people in their houses, it just wasn't the same. So, when Mother announced she was pregnant right before breakfast at Grandpa John's one morning, all the children were as happy as if it was the first baby ever.

"When will she be here?" Janessa asked.

"How do you know it'll be a girl? It might be a boy," Ted challenged.

"How do you know it won't be a girl?" Becca bantered.

"Children, let's not argue. We'll be happy whatever we have," Mother assured.

"Will we have it before we move into Father's house?" Tilly asked.

"I don't know, we still have a few months. We'll just have to see," Mother said sweetly.

Becca hadn't even noticed a baby belly. With Mother's long dresses, it was hard to tell, but she could see a bump had surfaced.

"When can we tell the rest of the family?" Becca wondered.

"Father wants to announce it tonight at the big house over Sunday dinner," Mother beamed.

Moans of protest polluted the air.

"That's hours away. How am I gonna to keep from telling Jerusha at church?" Becca said, flopping on the couch.

Clapping her hands together, Mother tried to motivate, "Come on everyone, we can do this. Let's get ready for church. It'll go by fast. Before you know it, we'll be eating with our whole family and letting them know about our newest little Johnson."

It was hard to complain while seeing her so happy. Tilly took the lead, "Yes, Mother, we can do this. Come on, let's get ready."

The other siblings followed, and Becca gave Mother a quick hug, rubbed her belly, and then ran to get her church supplies.

Becca sat next to Jerusha in Church while Uncle Fred spoke, but all she could think was…*we're going to have a new baby… we're going to have a new baby!*

Wanting it keep it a surprise, she tried extra hard to pay attention as a somber Uncle Fred explained how Uncle Warren would be the mouthpiece of his father, Uncle Rulon the prophet for a while.

Becca couldn't understand how the prophet could be sick enough to not come to church…he was supposed to live forever, but she listened to Uncle Fred speak with urgency.

"We must be vigilant in our deeds and prayers," Uncle Fred encouraged. "Surely our Prophet would not be sick if we were doing our part in being obedient, praying often and keeping the Holy Spirit.…"

Becca remembered her cousin, Sam, at the Golden Circle, and her dad. She couldn't help but wonder if their actions possibly had something to do with his sickness. For a moment, she felt guilty for even being around Travis, but then became very grateful to have Father Arlen. With a new baby coming, they needed a Father who held the priesthood and a prophet who was healthy. Becca promised herself to do better on behalf of the prophet.

When church was over, Becca linked her arm in Jerusha's and said, "You're riding with us!"

Since it was Mother Susan's week to cook, they were meeting up with the whole family at Father's big house. Becca loved it when they ate at Father's house. It was like a party playing with her cousins that were now brothers and sisters. And the food, oh the food. Sunday meals were always better than regular weeknight meals. Even though she felt a little weird around Mother Susan, she had to admit that her food was the best.

Unable to keep the surprise to herself once seated next to Jerusha in the van, Becca caved.

"Mother told us this morning we're gonna have a baby!" She whispered.

"That's so exciting! That way our new baby will have a friend!" Jerusha said excitedly.

"Your new baby? Mother Susan is going to have a baby?" Becca asked, clueless.

"Really soon. She kept it from us to be sure she doesn't lose it. She didn't want to get our hopes up if it didn't make it like some of the others," Jerusha explained.

It's not that it was horrible news, it was good. Two babies who could grow up together as friends was a sweet thing. They would be like twins. Becca was happy but couldn't help but feel a little less wind in her sail. Their baby wouldn't be the newest Johnson like Mother had said. She wondered if Mother knew.

"Our babies will be great friends!" Jerusha said.

"Yep, just like us!" Becca added.

Becca was nine when Janessa was born, and Mother had given birth at a hospital in Utah. At the Crick, Mothers usually delivered at the Hildale clinic. It was an add-on to Uncle Fred's humongous house. Almost mansion-like, his home was a hide-and-seeker's paradise because of its many hallways, bedrooms, and unexpected places to hide. It had to be big to hold all of Uncle Fred's wives and children, of which there were dozens. Aunt Lydia, his first wife, assisted with the births at the clinic with the help of other midwives. She wasn't a doctor, but she was well respected and had delivered and named many of the babies in the community.

Once girls reached a certain age, they could volunteer at the clinic under the guidance of a night nurse. Girls Becca's age could refill the mother's water jugs, get ice, and take food trays. She was still too young to help care for newborns but loved the idea of helping and being close to the sweet new babies. She had heard stories from Lea, one of her cousins who lived there and couldn't wait to experience it herself.

One day her mother and mother Susan surprised Becca and Jerusha by arranging a night for them to volunteer.

"Girls, you'll need to know that you'll be expected to stay awake all night. Do you think you can do that?" Mother Susan asked sternly.

"Yes," the girls answered in unison, barely able to keep still as they rode the short van ride to the clinic.

"How many babies are there right now?" Becca asked.

"I'm not sure. But Becca you're there to help the Mothers. Don't beg to hold the babies," Mother Susan instructed.

"I knooooow," Becca replied, a little more loudly than she had intended.

Jerusha looked at her and saw Mother Susan looking up at her in the rearview mirror. Becca didn't intend to not be sweet, it just came out a little sassy. Changing the subject, Becca said, "Thank you, Mother Susan, for bringing us."

"Just stay busy and don't get into trouble," She reminded.

Both girls nodded happily, and Becca's tone was forgotten.

Pine scent greeted them as Mother Susan opened the door to the clinic and the two giddy girls walked inside. Chairs lined the front room where family members could wait for babies to be born. Mother Susan walked the girls through the waiting room and down the hall to the birthing center, then introduced them to the night nurse who was waiting to give them instructions.

Pointing to a small kitchen area, the nurse said, "We have snacks and pitchers for ice water in here, and we pick up the new Mother's meals in the main kitchen at 5, then deliver them."

She raced down the hall, and the girls had to almost run to keep up with her as she took them down several different hallways, talking the whole time.

"You will help serve dinner and get them anything they need. After you've delivered their food, you can go back into the kitchen and make your own plates."

She finished just as they walked into the central kitchen where the evening plates were almost ready to be served.

Becca smelled something almost sweet cooking on the stove but couldn't quite make it out. It was thick, green and nearly made her gag. Thankfully, it was overpowered by the smell of fresh bread another mother was pulling out of the oven. Becca hadn't really thought about eating and now didn't look forward to it once she saw what it was.

The kitchen was like a well-oiled machine. Uncle Fred's wives alternated making meals for the clinic as well as for their own large family. Becca watched as the hard-working mothers and daughters scurried around the kitchen and couldn't help but be excited for the time when her whole family could do the same under one roof.

"Becca," She barely had time to turn before feeling a tap on her shoulder. It was her cousin, Lea. "I didn't know you were coming."

"It was a surprise for us, too," Becca exclaimed, hugging her back.

"You should come spend the night sometime. We could ride horses and catch bullfrogs in the pond at the community Zoo." She talked as she washed her hands, and then dried them on her apron.

"That sounds so fun," Becca accepted the invitation with great anticipation, genuinely excited to share time with Lea. Catching bullfrogs at the Zoo was one of her favorite things to do in the summertime.

"Come on, girls, we need to get dinner to the new mothers," the night Nurse reminded, and Lea stepped back to the sink to finish dishes.

As Becca and Jerusha headed back toward the birthing center, they noticed a rush of activity as a new mother was coming in to deliver.

Becca's heart began to race. They were going to be there for the delivery. The night just seemed to get better and better.

Giddier because of the new development, the girls worked quickly to deliver dinners and check on the resting mothers and their tiny babies. Both babies were girls, and cute as everything. Becca loved the slow movements of a newborn and wished she could hold one but didn't dare ask. Instead, she inquired as professionally as she would at the Golden Circle, "How's the soup?"

Both mothers seemed to love the soup, so as Becca and Jerusha dished up their own back in the kitchen, they were cautiously optimistic. It was split pea. In unison, Becca and Jerusha lifted their spoons to taste the goo, and quickly decided to just focus on the bread instead.

"If I was having a baby, then I think I'd want something different, like a Monte Cristo," Becca said as they finished their bread.

"What's a Monte Cristo?" Jerusha asked.

"It's a French toast sandwich with meat, and melted cheese dipped in yogurt. We make them at The Golden Circle," Becca answered as they washed the dishes.

"Is it ever scary working at the Golden Circle with all those apostates coming in?" Jerusha asked.

"It's not scary. I have Uncle Seth and Levi there, and Stacy and I have so much fun. Most of the people are very nice." She remembered the older couple who would clap for her and smiled. "If you're nice to them, they give bigger tips."

It had been at least an hour since the girls had seen any night nurses because they were all busy with the new delivery. Becca and Jerusha checked on the other two babies but both moms were fine and didn't need a thing. It would have been fun to go back to the main house and visit with Lea, but Becca knew that was for another time. For all of the expected excitement, they were bored with the wait.

"I wonder if we should take dinner to the mother in delivery," Becca said, antsy to know any news.

Always cautious, Jerusha answered, "I don't know. I don't want to go without asking the night nurse."

"Well, I'm going to go ask," Becca decided and walked down two hallways to find a room with a light on. Jerusha followed cautiously.

The room had two twin beds, and opposite the beds was a wall with a huge mirror on it. Next to the mirror was a closed door where Becca could hear someone talking calmly saying, "You're doing great. Just one more push."

Then, interrupting the calm, was a soft baby cry. Goosebumps covered her arms as Becca turned toward Jerusha with a satisfied grin. Becca walked half way to the door. It opened, and one of the Midwives walked out, leaving the door open. Both Becca and the Midwife jumped, startled by each other's presence, and Jerusha nearly fell. Becca wasn't close enough to investigate the room but could see reflected in the mirror, a bundle of goo, and an enormous amount of blood.

"Becca, Jerusha, you scared me!" She scolded.

"We just came to see if the new mother wanted any food," Becca tried to sound professional, but she felt anything but professional as she thought about all the blood reflected in the mirror.

The Midwife closed the door to the delivery room, grabbed some towels and said, "Not yet, she just delivered. I'll be taking care of her tonight."

Nodding her head, Becca said, "OK" and walked out as if she were calm as a bird with Jerusha in tow. Once they were down the hallway, they quickened their pace to find a place to sit and process through what they had just seen. Neither girl spoke, but Becca knew they were thinking the same thing.

Why was there so much blood and where did it come from?

***

A few weeks later, as Tilly and Becca walked up to the house after school, Janessa ran outside yelling, "Mother Susan had her baby, Mother Susan had her baby."

Tilly and Becca put their school bags down inside the doorway, and Mother joined them.

"Hi girls, let's get to the van. We have a new sister to meet."

Becca and Tilly looked at each other and squealed. It was a girl.

"What's her name?" Tilly asked as they approached the clinic.

"Arnella, after Father Arlen," Mother answered.

Tilly said, "Oh, how sweet. I've never heard that name before."

That's the weirdest name for a girl! Becca thought it, but refrained from sharing, smiling in agreement with Tilly and then asked, "Do you think Mother Susan would let me hold her?"

"Now, Becca, I know how you love to hold babies, but this time why don't you just wait til Mother Susan asks you," Mother suggested.

"Ok," Becca said it with good manners, but was still disappointed. Mother had let all her brothers and sisters hold Janessa the day she was born.

"I wish I could've seen her be born," Tilly said as they walked into the waiting area at the clinic.

"Not me," Becca informed, remembering the blood and how she felt after seeing it, "I've been close enough to a baby being born."

"Well, I haven't," Tilly maintained.

Minutes later, Father Arlen, Mother Susan holding baby Arnella, and Jerusha entered the waiting room. Becca recognized the night nurse who had been there the night she volunteered weeks earlier.

"Thought we'd come to you," she explained, "Those rooms are just too small to have the whole family back."

Mother Susan handed Arnella to Jerusha once she was seated and said, "Here's baby Arnella."

"Awe, she's so cute." The girls gathered around, soaking in the excitement of their new little sister and touching her tiny fingers.

Mother walked to Mother Susan's side, and the two visited through whispers.

After about 10 minutes, Mother joined the girls and said, "We can't stay too long, Mother Susan's had a long day."

They had just gotten there. Becca started to say something, but Tilly gave her a you-better-not look, so she just kept quiet.

On the way home, Becca felt weird. She had been so excited to see her new baby sister but left the clinic feeling something she couldn't quite understand. Jerusha had been allowed to stay, and no one else had been able to hold the baby. Somehow it didn't feel like she had a new sister at all, even though she did.

***

Every day brought them closer to the house being finished, and the whole family coming together, but as the days and weeks passed, they all knew it wouldn't be ready before Mother had her baby.

It was summertime, and Becca was bored and tired of waiting. She barely even got to see little Arnella, and when she did see her on Sundays, Mother Susan wasn't very open to the other kids holding her. Weekends were busy with work on Saturdays and the usual Sunday responsibilities, but weekdays left her restless, ready for a change. Thankfully, after her encounter with her cousin, Lea, at the clinic, Becca had been invited to play with Lea several times. They rode horses, played hide-and-seek, and caught giant bullfrogs at the Community Zoo pond. It kept her mind and body busy, and she was grateful to have something to do.

Becca felt very important when she was at Uncle Fred's house filled with girls and mothers who kept busy sewing, cleaning, cooking and caring for the women in their community.

One time, Becca was invited to go on a big trip to Phoenix with Uncle Fred's family. Becca's Aunt who was Lea's mother, called the girls in to be fitted for matching dresses. All the girls would match and would be easy to spot in a crowd. It reminded Becca of the closeness she felt to her cousin, Desiree and more than ever, the Crick felt like home.

***

"Arlinda?" Becca questioned making sure she heard it correctly.

"Yep, after Father Arlen," Mother Claudia explained.

Her little sister was finally born.

Processing the name, Becca tried not to sound disrespectful, after all, this was her baby sister. It was only right that she be named after Father Arlen if the other baby had. In a way it would be more like twins. But still, they were such weird names. Arlinda and Arnella.

Brown eyes dotted Arlinda's perfect, round face. Becca loved to hold her tiny bundled sister. It was as if the world had begun again. Becca was in love. The older children were allowed to give her baths and dress her, and she quickly became the most exciting person in Grandfather John's house.

Becca still went to Lea's on occasion but wanted to enjoy her new baby sister as much as she could, so she stayed home more to help prepare for the big move.

One day Father Arlen took the older girls to the hardware store to order carpet for the room Tilly, Jerusha, and Becca would share. Fresh carpet smell hung in the air as they turned through the carpet samples. Once the purple sample was turned, it was all over. All three girls gasped and agreed. Father Arlen was so pleased with their cooperation, he took them to see how their room was progressing.

Pressed wood siding that matched the other unfinished houses at the Crick greeted them as they walked up to their newly remodeled, enormous home. Father opened the front door, and Becca breathed in the musty smell of freshly dry-walled sheetrock.

Excited to see the new space they would share, the girls bustled up the wooden, unfinished stairs. Becca was the first inside their room, "Oh my goodness! We have a sink with another mirror in our room! And look, we have our own walk-in closet!"

Tilly and Jerusha gasped, and Tilly started making plans. "My bed will go over there, and my dresser there..."

That was so like Tilly to start marking her territory.

What makes her think she just gets to take over?

She was the oldest but didn't have the right to always to have her way.

"Let's wait and see how it all fits," Becca suggested, trying to keep things fair.

Jerusha didn't say a word. She would do whatever anyone told her. Ignoring Tilly's sour face, Becca walked out of the room to investigate the rest of the house.

She counted thirteen bedrooms and nine bathrooms. Each of the three mothers had their own rooms with private bathrooms. Each mother's room had a unique feature. Mother Claudia got a bay window and a jetted tub. Mother Susan got double doors to the back porch, and Becca's Mother got double doors out the second story balcony. Father

Arlen didn't have his own room as he would just alternate and share rooms with each of the mothers. That left ten bedrooms for twenty-four children. It was a little bit bigger than Grandfather John's two-story where they lived, but they needed every inch of it for their big family. Her favorite part was the balcony she and her sisters would share. If she needed a little space, she could just go outside.

If someone had told her three years ago they would be living like this, she wouldn't have believed it. Three Mothers, an enormous house, and twenty-three brothers and sisters made her feel as if they were as important as Uncle Fred's family.

***

"I'm sorry it bothers you. Just look away," Mother urged.

"But Mother, she just leaves everything out, and it's right in front of us while we eat," Ted countered.

"We are taught to not look at girls. The prophet said so," Benjamin reasoned.

"Mother Susan isn't a girl, she's a Mother," Tilly chimed in to support Mother.

"But it's her girl parts. We don't want to see that, Mother. We don't see you when you feed Arlinda, you cover up with a blanket."

"I understand, I wish she wouldn't do that in front of you. Maybe I can ask Father Arlen to speak to her about just covering up at the dinner table because it makes you boys feel uncomfortable," she said.

Becca listened as the boys explained their concerns to Mother. All of Becca's brothers and sisters had been shocked when, at Sunday dinner, Mother Susan had exposed her chest at the dinner table to feed sweet Arnella. It was a beautiful thing that Mothers could feed babies that way and Becca was *fascinated* with the idea, but had to admit, it left her feeling weird too. They were taught all their lives that seeing another person under their garments was a bad thing. Confused, Becca wondered how her mother couldn't feel the same way.

Surely the prophet would not approve of them seeing Mother Susan where her garments should cover.

The very next Sunday as they met around the table, Becca was quite relieved as was Ted, Benjamin, and Justin when Mother Susan had a blanket over her shoulder as she fed Arnella. Her scowl told another story, though, and as the meal went on, Becca couldn't help but notice Mother Susan seemed like she was getting angry as she fumbled to eat and keep covered.

In no time at all, Mother Susan turned, tossed the blanket aside and looked up at the children as if to dare them to look. All of the boys immediately buried their faces in their plates and kept their eyes on their food. Becca glanced at her Mother who held a smile on her face like she hadn't a care in the world.

7

GOING TO COURT AND GETTING A NEW BIKE
1997

"Children you won't be going to school tomorrow. We have to go to St. George for a court hearing." Mother announced Sunday evening after family prayer.

"What's a court hearing?" Ted asked.

"It's just a place where we talk to a judge," Mother answered.

"What's a Judge?" Justin continued.

"He's a man who will take you in a room and ask you questions. You don't have to do anything but answer his questions truthfully," Mother encouraged.

"What kind of questions?" Janessa wondered.

"My Lanta, hopefully not as many as you children, now go to bed," she said motioning upstairs.

The next morning Becca and her blood brothers and sisters filled the big van and rode to St. George with Mother and Father. She usually loved any adventure that took her anywhere new but found herself nervous and fidgety as she sat in the quiet, formal courtroom. Sitting still was her least favorite thing to do, and now, with dead silence and nothing to do, all she could do was think.

She was frustrated. The last two days had been torture. On Saturday Tilly had gotten up with her at 4:30 and informed her that she was going to work with Uncle Seth at the Golden Circle. The drive to Hurricane had been unbearable. Becca liked having Uncle Seth, Levi, and Stacy to herself. Tilly's presence made her job seem more like a job than the fun getaway it had become. To top it all off, she had to split her tips, and that just felt wrong.

It weighed heavily on Becca's heart. The Golden Circle was hers. It would be different if she and Tilly were close, but for some reason, they never saw eye to eye. No matter what idea Becca came up with, Tilly found a way to take it over and then treat Becca like it was hers.

A door opened and shocked her back to the present. To her surprise, her dad and a man in a long robe approached them. She didn't realize dad would be there. He was wearing a short-sleeved shirt. Seeing him in gentile clothing was always hard, but as he smiled warmly at Becca and the older kids, her heart was put to ease. He glanced at their Mother, who was holding little Arlinda. It was his first time to see her. Becca didn't recognize the look in his eye and noticed Mother turn her attention toward the window.

It always felt different to see him outside of the community. At the Crick, he was just an apostate, someone to be tolerated and cautioned about. But in that room, he was more like a dad. She just couldn't understand why he didn't seem excited to see Arlinda. It almost felt like he was ignoring her.

One by one, the judge called each of the children back into his book-lined office. Becca wished she could ask them what they talked about, but it was too quiet to feel comfortable to speak in the waiting room. She couldn't imagine what a man in a robe would ask her about.

When it was Becca's turn to see him, she was surprised to find he was friendlier than she had imagined and only asked her straightforward questions about how she liked visiting her dad. In that room, away from the Crick and anyone else to hear, she felt very comfortable telling the truth. She enjoyed being with her dad. He was an apostate but was always good to them.

After what seemed like forever, the judge finished talking to all the children and then asked Mother and Travis into his office. Tilly held baby Arlinda, and Father Arlen stayed with the children. Becca tried to entertain herself by playing with Arlinda, but Tilly turned her eyebrows down and told her to be still. Ted and Benjamin were acting like goofballs, but she said nothing to them.

To her right was a table filled with magazines. They looked decent enough, nothing like the magazine she saw in Riverton. One on top had a picture of a beautiful dessert and said, "Recipe page 115." She reached to pick it up but heard Father Arlen clear his throat loudly. Turning to his gaze, Becca met his eyes, and he shook his head. It was a cooking magazine. How could it be bad? Her dad would not have cared if she looked at a cooking magazine. She knew Father meant well, but it was a *cooking* magazine. Wound up tighter than Mother Susan's braid, Becca put her hands in her lap and sat.

Thankfully, her Mother returned shortly, and the family left the stifling waiting room. Restless from the day of sitting and silence, the children were moody and short with each other on the drive home. Even Tilly's blatant reminders to keep sweet fell on deaf ears. Mother seemed uncharacteristically tense, and Father seemed concerned.

All Becca could think about was riding a bike. Freedom was calling, and there was nothing like a ride when she felt that way. It was too bad Ted's bike was the only one that fit her; borrowing his bike was next to impossible, even if he wasn't using it. She refused to ride her own bike because it was too small. Janessa had inherited it months earlier because when Becca tried to ride, she looked plain-old stupid with her knees up to her elbows. She felt like a clown in a parade, and that was not a good feeling.

Once they were home, she purposely waited until Ted and Benjamin were busy rollerblading to ask.

"Can I use your bike?"

"I might need it in a minute," Ted said without a thought.

"Awe, come on Ted, you're rollerbladin', and I won't be gone very long," she reasoned.

"Nope. I might need it in a minute, and you won't be here with it," he said.

It was no use. Once Ted made up his mind there was no changing it.

"Fine!" Becca said and then stomped off to put her rollerblades on. They would have to do.

She had asked dad to get a bike that would fit her the last time he had visited. So far, he had told her no. He had reasoned that the children had not taken care of the other toys he bought so he wouldn't get them anything new until they were old enough to take better care of things. At the time, Becca had felt almost angry that an apostate, of all people, could tell her about how to behave. But right then she wished she had taken better care of her old bike, and maybe dad would have gotten her a new one.

Before she could take off riding her blades, Mother came outside and stood on the step.

"My children come here," she called. "Travis will be over soon and is asking if you want to go get sandwiches at the Candy Shop. You don't have to go, but if you choose to, he will be here soon."

"I already saw Travis today," Tilly said and walked inside.

"I'll go!" Becca said.

Excited for sandwiches and the chance to talk to him about a bike, Becca hopped up to go inside to comb her hair and wash her hands. Becca needed to convince him that she had learned her lesson about taking good care of her toys so she would have one thing to solely call her own. Tilly had taken The Golden Circle from her, and Ted wouldn't share the only thing that gave her a sense of freedom. Between losing both of those freedoms, Becca was feeling desperate to be heard and understood.

Travis drove up, and Ted and Benjamin wasted no time jumping in with him, then fought for the front seat. Becca, Janessa, and Justin jumped in just as mother said, "Tomorrow is a school day. Have them home soon."

"I know. They're my children, too," Travis returned.

Becca looked up from buckling when she heard him say those four words. *They're my children too.*

All this time she hadn't considered he could say that. They had a Father who held the priesthood. Father Arlen was her new Father. She knew the prophet would not approve, but it was true. They were his children too.

Becca looked out the car window and noticed several of her other siblings standing outside staring at Travis with disapproval. For a moment, she felt guilty for going with him but reminded herself that she needed to talk about a bike.

"How about we grab dinner and take it to Cottonwood Park? You all probably need to get out and run," Dad suggested.

Relieved, the children agreed heartily. Once they ate and everyone else went off to play, Becca stayed behind and sat on the picnic table with her dad.

"Tilly started working at The Golden Circle," she began.

"Really. How's that going?" He said.

"Well, it makes me mad. The Golden Circle was my job first, and I'm really good at it. She always takes over everything. Ted takes over everything too. I just want somethin' for me." She looked up to see if he was following. His face gave away no clues, so she continued.

"I know you say we haven't taken care of our things, but I really want a bike. It's the only way I can do somethin' by myself. I promise I will take care of it. I won't let anyone else ride it. I'll clean it and put it away. Please, please could you get me one?" She said, looking straight into his face.

"Becca, a bike costs a lot of money. And money doesn't just fall off trees. I have to work hard for that money," he said.

"I know, I know. I would buy it myself if my money from the Golden Circle could be mine, but I'm supposed to turn it into Father to help with our new house. I know how you have to work for money. I promise I will take better care of it." She said, her hazel eyes twinkling. She felt so ready to take on the responsibility of a bike.

"I'll think about it and decide before I see you again."

Wanting to seem grateful, and not naggy, Becca changed the subject, "Weren't you happy to see Arlinda?"

He was quiet for a while like he was thinking. "Well, I was happier to see you and your brothers and sisters that's all."

"Mother Susan had a baby too. Her name is Arnella. It's a little weird, but it gets better every time I say it. They are named after Father Arlen," Becca rambled.

Dad faced forward, starring off into the distance, and then turned to her and said, "You know what makes me happy? I get to take you all every other Christmas to Utah."

"We can go to Utah with you for Christmas?" Becca questioned.

"Yep, the judge said so," he said.

They had only celebrated Christmas once since moving to Grandpa John's at the Crick. For some reason, the Prophet decided it wasn't necessary, so they stopped. The idea of celebrating Christmas was exciting but felt weird all at the same time.

"Well then, if the judge said so, then I guess it'll be ok with the Prophet," Becca said.

"Yep, it's better than ok," Dad said with a big smile. "I need to get going. Let's go get your brothers and sister. I have a four-hour drive home and some thinking to do about a bike."

"What about this one?" Dad pointed to a pink bike with flowers.

"It's pretty," Becca said, "But I was thinkin' one with lots of color like this."

She pointed to a bright neon green bike.

"Go ahead and try it out," Dad encouraged.

Becca hopped on, careful to fold her long dress so it wouldn't get caught in the spokes and pushed off in the aisle of the store. It was perfect. Her legs could bend, and she could sit up straight. Imagining riding all over the Crick gave her a sense of importance, and she ignored anyone who looked her way as she walked the bike back toward her dad in the huge store.

Grinning, he said, "Looks like you've found one."

As they walked up to pay, he reminded her, "Remember Becca, I'll only buy this if you promise to take good care of it. I've worked to pay for it, now you've gotta work to take care of it."

"I will. I promise."

Because the Judge had said they could visit Travis regularly, Becca felt a trust for him that had been absent for some time. He was an apostate, but he was her dad. The prophet would not approve, but with the Judge's approval, Becca felt better about going with him, especially when she wanted something. For a moment she felt sad that her main reasoning for going to visit him was to ask him to get a bike, but at the same time, she could not deny her growing admiration. He kept coming back, even when they pushed him away.

Several brothers and sisters were rollerblading and playing on the porch as she and her dad parked. Before the engine had even turned off, they scurried into the house. Dad took out the bike, and Becca spoke up one last time.

"Thank you, Dad. I'll take care of it, I promise."

"You're welcome. I love you." He patted her shoulder and then motioned to the bike, "Now go have fun."

When he was far enough away, all of her siblings but Tilly came back outside.

As if reporting breaking news, Becca squared her shoulders and declared to anyone who could hear, "This is my bike, and I promised my dad that no one else would ride it. He got it for me, and I have to take care of it."

No one said a thing and Becca couldn't tell what they were thinking. It didn't matter anyway. She had a bike.

***

"We're home, Becca," Tilly wiggled Becca's shoulder as Uncle Seth turned off the truck. It was almost midnight, and she had fallen asleep on the drive home from a long, busy day at The Golden Circle. Gathering her things, Becca groggily opened her eyes and then noticed a van outside Grandpa John's house.

Recognizing it, Becca was instantly awake and excited. It was Desiree's family. She jumped up and made her way inside not waiting for anyone else to follow. Everyone was asleep. It tortured her to know that Desiree was upstairs, rooms away without being able to talk. Fighting the urge to romp upstairs to Grandma Leah's level and wake her cousin with a big fat hug, she forced herself to go to bed, determined to get up early and surprise her at a more appropriate time.

Just as the sun peaked up, Becca bounded upstairs and plopped down on the bed next to her sleeping cousin. "Desiree! Wake up!"

"Hi to you too, stranger," Desiree teased as she struggled to open her eyes.

Becca laughed and gave her a hug, "How long are you stayin'?"

"We're only here for the weekend, but we'll be comin' back every weekend for a while." Sitting up proudly, she finished, "Father is building us a house."

"What? You're gonna live here?" Unable to fathom the idea, Becca smacked Desiree on the head with a pillow.

"Stop, you'll mess up my lovely head…" Desiree teased, reaching her hand to her messy head as if to smooth a perfect hairdo, "…and by the way, you'd get to see me more if you weren't working at The Golden Circle every Saturday," Desiree continued.

"Oh, I didn't think about that," Becca was both excited and disappointed at the same time. "But when you live here, I'll see you all the time. Maybe you can even work at the Golden Circle with me."

"Well, I don't know. My mother needs lots of help. She's gonna have twins!" Desiree shared.

"Twins! Oh. My. Gosh. You're so lucky! Twin babies, just like Benjamin and me!"

"But Father says it'll take at least a year to finish the house because we can only do it on the weekends. We'll be here for sure before 2000."

Just the mention of the year 2000 made Becca shudder. It was something she did not like to think about. Prophecies warning of the events of the coming turn of the century had been a source of fear for years. Everyone at the Crick was preparing, well in advance and Becca was glad to know her cousin would be safe and sound at the Crick soon.

"Well, it's about time you guys moved here!" Becca teased, lightening the mood.

"Hey, why don't you come down to Grandma Claudia's kitchen to hang out with us and eat coffee cake before church," Becca suggested.

"If I feel like it," Desiree said, flopping back into bed and pulling the covers over her head.

Becca grabbed a pillow, whopped Desiree on the head again and said, "You do look like you need some more beauty sleep."

It felt like old times. Becca couldn't wait til Desiree was back within pillow-whopping reach for good and safe from any outside harm.

8

A NEW KIND OF TROUBLE
1997

CODE OF CONDUCT: SISTER WIVES

Be careful not to have other friendships with other girls once you are married. Holding onto other friendships will hinder you from bonding with your sister wives. They must be your best friends because they belong to your husband. Girls must be prepared for this in their father's home. Girls are to love all their mothers and call them mother.

"We have purple carpet," Becca hummed as she carried a box to the new room that she, Jerusha, and Tilly would share. Tilly was right behind her with a box of her own, wearing a satisfied grin. Both girls had taken Saturday off from The Golden Circle to help move into their new house. Uncles and aunts pitched in to help as well, so in no time at all, Becca's family was all settled into their much anticipated remodeled home.

Several priesthood men gathered in the living room and dedicated the enormous house with prayer. Afterwards, cousins went with cousins to decorate and organize. It was like they were living in their own hotel.

Becca's heart was full of gratitude, and she vowed to keep sweet as she went to bed that night. All her Mothers and siblings were safe, sound, and secured under one roof, and she admired Father for bringing them all together.

Becca's feeling of security was rocked though, when just weeks after they moved in, Uncle Warren announced to the community that the Prophet's health was failing. His sickness signaled something was about to happen in the heavens, and disaster was on its way far before the anticipated year 2000, which would bring every form of darkness known to man. Everyone was encouraged more than ever to pray and keep sweet. Believers in Canada, Utah, Texas, and the Crick went into prayer mode.

Great earthquakes, fires, and famine were predicted. Leaving the Crick was not an option. If believers left, they would not be protected from the wrath that was coming. With every week that passed, Becca grew more and more concerned for those who practiced their faith and lived off the Crick. Thankful Desiree's family was at least building a house, she tried not to think about what would happen if the house was not finished.

Fear spread as fast as the news and everywhere Becca went, she noticed people smiling a little more and behaving a little sweeter to one other. Aware of the importance of being lifted up, children tried more than ever to obey their mothers and fathers.

While they were confident they were the chosen people, it didn't hurt to be extra sure. So, when the time came for the children to go with Travis for a visit, it was out of the question. Mother left it up to them to decide, but there was no way any child wanted to be away from the Crick. Terrified, even Becca wanted nothing to do with a visit.

As the weeks and months went by with no signs of the prophecies coming true, the whole community seemed to relax as the Prophet's health improved. It was though their sweetness had kept the predictions from happening. Once the imminent danger seemed to have passed, Mother allowed the children to go on a short overnight visit with Travis to St. George.

Although Becca was a little weary, she rationalized that St. George was way closer than Riverton, and if anything happened, surely Travis could get them back in time.

The brief visit went by without any disasters, and Becca happily returned home with a can of soda and some treats to put in the fridge for later. She noticed her siblings from other mothers looking at her with suspicion like she had gone and robbed a store or something.

"What? It's just a soda. Don't drink it, though, it's mine!" She warned them and closed the fridge.

"What'd you do with Travis?" Mother Claudia asked.

"Just mostly hung out in the hotel and ate pizza." Becca smiled up at Mother Claudia. She knew better than to tell her they went swimming and then watched television in the hotel *while* they ate pizza. Besides, other siblings were listening, and she didn't want to make them feel bad.

"Did you remember your prayers?" She asked.

"Yep," she assured.

"Now, I know hotels have TVs. I hope you didn't watch something the Prophet wouldn't approve of," she fished for more information.

"We were good. Dad doesn't let us watch anything bad," Becca answered respectfully. Other than her own Mother, Becca liked Mother Claudia best. Mother Susan had heard the whole exchange and didn't say a word to Becca but went into the next room.

Becca looked at Mother Claudia and shrugged her shoulders. She really wanted to love mother Susan but seemed to always do something that made her upset. It reminded her of Tilly. No matter what she did, somehow Becca was always doing something wrong. It was exhausting to try and figure it out, so she decided to go play.

After going with Travis, it always felt good to go outside and rollerblade or ride her bike amongst the red rocks of home. She decided to roller blade but couldn't find them.

"Jerusha, have you seen my roller blades?" she asked.

"You might check with Casey."

"Why with Casey?" Becca asked.

"Well, I saw Casey with them yesterday," Jerusha confided.

Why would Casey think she could use my blades? Everyone knew Becca had made it obvious that no one was allowed to use her stuff. She liked to take care of her things. When the other children used her toys, they tore them up and left them outside like trash.

"Casey, do you know where my blades are?" Becca confronted.

"No, why would I know?" she answered. Becca had the feeling she knew more, but couldn't prove it, so she just went room to room looking and asking as anger started to gather more and more momentum.

Once every nook and cranny was checked without any luck, Becca asked Jerusha one more time if she had any ideas. Jerusha nervously admitted she may have seen them in Mother Susan's room.

Boldly, Becca went to Mother Susan's door and knocked.

"Come in," she said.

"Mother Susan, do you know where my roller blades are?" Becca asked.

"No, are they not where you put them last?" She answered.

"I did put them where I always do, and they're not there. Jerusha told me Casey wore 'em yesterday when I was with my dad," Becca said.

"Well, I don't think so," Mother Susan answered with a blank expression.

Before she left, Becca couldn't help but notice a can of soda on Mother Susan's bedside table. It was the same flavor she had put in the fridge just hours before.

She ran down to the fridge. It was gone. Mother Susan had taken her soda. Jerusha had not made up what she had seen. Becca knew Mother Susan had to know more. If she would take her drink, then she had no intentions of respecting anything of Becca's.

Later that night when Mother Susan was in the shower, Becca snuck into her room to investigate. Lifting blankets, she searched under the bed and then sifted through some piles of clothes before opening the closet door. Smack dab in front of her was her roller blades. They were distinctly marked, *Becca Johnson*. Mother Susan had to know they were Becca's, and she had to know they were there.

Grabbing them, Becca marched into Mother's room to tell her about what had happened. Mother listened patiently with concern as Becca related the entire story. Once Becca finished, Mother said, "Well we just have to love her and pray we can have peace with it."

"But she took my soda!" Becca said, exasperated that her Mother would just ignore the offense.

"I'm sorry Becca. That wasn't kind of her, but you really shouldn't be goin' into Mother Susan's room either."

Clamping her lips tightly to keep sweet, Becca said, "But Mother, she lied and then stole. I would get into so much trouble if I did that!"

"Mother Susan loves you, and I know you love her too. She is my sister wife and, in time, will become one of my best friends. Friends forgive each other."

A different emotion washed over Becca. How could her sweet mother choose Mother Susan's side? None of it came close to making sense. Becca left her mother's room and hid the blades under her own bed, satisfied to know Mother Susan would be shocked when she discovered they were missing.

After school the next day, Becca couldn't wait to rollerblade and wondered if Mother Susan had noticed her empty closet. Proud as a pickle, Becca circled the carport, happy to have her belongings secured and in working order. With a nervous belly, she waited for Mother Susan to notice.

Sure enough, after a bit, Mother Susan walked outside and stared at Becca's scandalous feet. Straight-faced, she whirled around and went back into the house. A few minutes later, she tornadoed by with several of the other children in tow.

"Where you guys goin'?" Becca asked.

"We're going to the dairy to get some ice cream." Mother Susan reported.

"Oh, I want to go!" Becca said and started to remove her rollerblades.

"I think you had enough sweets when you went with your dad." Mother Susan said as all the younger siblings got into the van and left an open-mouthed Becca standing there with one blade on and one blade off.

***

Careful to keep her extra high, braided hair undisturbed, Becca delicately pulled on her new dress over her longies, then adjusted the tip of the braid that was punctuated with a purple scrunchie. Next, she put on a pair of leggings, then tugged on a thick pair of pantyhose over those, and last, finished off with a thin pair of hose.

Layering two pairs of hose was laborious, but it camouflaged the seams of her longies and leggings, making her legs look smooth. Not that anyone would even see her legs, but she knew they looked polished, and that was enough for her. It was a lot of work, but she loved getting ready for a community dance.

Although some people frowned on the tradition, Uncle Fred oversaw the dances and enjoyed watching the young teens dance and enjoy themselves. As long as rules were followed, the leaders of the community would allow the tradition to continue.

Girls would sit in chairs with their backs to the boys with their feet crossed. Boys would tap a girl on the shoulder if they wanted to dance. Usually, there was no conversation while Great Grandmother Verna played the piano and the pair waltzed. Hawk-like, the elders in the community kept a close watch for any immoral behaviors.

Becca loved to waltz and never understood why parents had to be so protective. It was true that she would have to touch a boy's hand, but they were just dancing. She allowed herself to forget that boys were snakes on the nights of community dances and let herself enjoy the satisfaction of moving with the music.

Upon arrival, Becca made her way to find a place next to someone she knew. Shirley, Stacy's sister, had an extra seat beside her, so Becca sat down and waited for the piano to begin.

"Hi Shirley, I like your dress." She said, admiring the pink taffeta cloth.

From the corner of her eye, Becca noticed there was something stuck to Shirley's lower leg. It looked like a loose hair had gotten woven into her pantyhose. That just wouldn't do. She reached down to pull it out and realized there was more than one.

"What are you doing?" Shirley said with a questioning look.

Realizing the hair wasn't loose, Becca retracted her hand. Shirley's leg hairs were longer than baby Arlinda's head hair. And they were sticking clear through two pairs of pantyhose and a pair of longies.

Embarrassed and a little shocked, Becca quickly recovered. "Oh, there was a string on you. I got it off, though."

Shirley was seventeen. Becca wondered if that was what was going to happen to her when she turned seventeen. No one had told her anything about leg hairs growing like that. She had never noticed any on Tilly or Mother. But then they never took their longies off in front of her so for all she knew, Tilly could have legs just like Shirley.

Becca had some short hairs on her legs, but they were like peach fuzz. The very thought made her want to cry. In just three years, she could have hair on her legs like an animal.

For the rest of the dance, Becca could hardly enjoy herself as she obsessed about what to do so her legs wouldn't get like Shirley's. Women were to keep their head hair long as a part of their religion, but she had never realized that meant leg hairs as well. Until seeing Shirley's legs, she didn't even know that might be a problem. It was a vain concern, but one she was willing to investigate a little further to find a solution.

Her own dad shaved his face hairs, so she thought, maybe he would help.

***

Weeks later, Becca was barefoot on the sand, holding Janessa's hand. Inhaling the salty air and watching the waves dance in the afternoon sun, she knew she had made the right decision to go on vacation with Travis to California.

For two weeks she had gone back and forth, trying to decide if it was worth the risk. Another prophecy had been made; terrible events were supposed to happen soon, and her fear of leaving the Crick was heightened.

Uncle Warren had declared via telecast from Utah that all faithful believers must pray harder than ever because the end of the world was at hand. The tragedy was supposed to happen in September, and it was August. Everyone was encouraged to keep sweet and follow the Holy Spirit ever so carefully to be protected from the wrath to come.

It mirrored the same prophecy delivered right after they moved into their house. And, while it was true that Travis did not hold the priesthood, therefore was unable to protect her from wrath, she had an urgent matter that needed to be handled. No one else was going to be able to do it except him.

Closing her eyes, listening to the water and happy ocean birds, she recalled the events that led her to change her mind.

> "If Travis held the priesthood it'd be different," Mother Susan cautioned as the girls hand-sewed repairs to their longies.
>
> *She doesn't have to point out the obvious.* Becca thought. *Why does mother Susan even bother? She only really cares about her blood children.*
>
> Recalling the ice-cream-roller-blade incident, Becca didn't care to hear Mother Susan's opinion.
>
> "It's up to the children if they want to see Travis. We just have to remember the prophet's words and count the cost. Evil is real, and you have no protection there. You

also have to bear in mind that you're an example for all of the other children. But in the end, it's your choice," Mother said.

Ted and Benjamin had it easy. They had to do Saturday work projects, so it was a given that they wouldn't go. Tilly always wanted to stay. She was more interested in pleasing Father and the prophet than wanting to leave the Crick with Travis. It was easy for her to say no. And truth be told, it was way better without Tilly. Becca wanted to say no, but there was always a small thread that somehow connected her to him, even though he was an apostate. Plus, she needed to talk to him about something.

Bringing the thread up to her teeth to cut her mending needle from the longies, Becca had a revelation. That's it! Her longies! They would protect her. She just wouldn't take them off.

"I'll go," Becca said.

"Me too, me too," Janessa followed.

At first Mother Susan acted like she was going to say something, with her mouth wide and eyebrows drawn, but instead sat motionless, holding her sewing needle midair.

Before Mother could say anything, Becca picked up Janessa and her mended longies. "Come on Janessa. We have some packing to do."

Eyes still closed, Becca heard her dad on the beach speaking in a quiet voice just where she could hear, "Are you sure you want to keep dressed in your regular clothes? I brought some different things just in case you want to change your mind."

Of course, she didn't want to change her mind. She was safer in her longies covered by her leggings and a long-sleeved t-shirt. Travis wouldn't understand. After all, he was an apostate. He wasn't allowed to wear longies anymore, but she was, and she wasn't about to take them off.

Let the other people run around exposed looking stupid.

"Nope, I'm good Trav…Dad."

She smiled, ran to the waves, and jumped bravely into the icy ocean. It was the first time she had used the word dad in months, and it felt like putting on her favorite old shoes that didn't quite fit anymore. Weird.

Janessa followed her into the water, and they squealed and shivered. Shocked by the cold, Janessa jumped onto Becca like a bear on a tree. It was late summertime, but the water wasn't like that of a swimming pool. It was cold and had a mind of its own. Giggling, Becca encouraged Janessa to get down and move.

"Let's try to jump the waves!" Janessa gasped.

"Ok, but let's hold hands," Becca said, grabbing her sister's tiny, icy fingers.

"1, 2, 3…JUMP!" and they leaped over the lazy waves.

Everything in the world stopped, and the only thing that mattered was jumping over those waves with her little sister. Even Dad joined them in the water and jumped. If she could, Becca would live next to the ocean and do this every day.

She felt completely free, except for one thing. Her clothes. Her leggings, which covered her longies, were holding a lot of water and making them droopy, sticky and cold. Looking down, she realized that, although the leggings did cover her, they were a little see-through and the impression of her longies was very apparent. Anyone around could see her underwear. At first, she tried just to ignore the awkward appearance of the soggy garments and have fun. Self-conscious though, she sunk further and further into the ocean, wanting to be fully covered by the water.

"Come on Becca. I want to jump!" Janessa bubbled.

"I'll jump with you," Dad broke in, allowing Becca to do her own thing.

Standing in the deeper water by herself, Becca was amused by her sister's joy, and her dad's eagerness to play but wished she could join their free-spirited fun.

"I have to go to the bathroom," Janessa announced, dancing around.

"Just go in the ocean," Dad whispered.

"Not that kind," Janessa whimpered, looking at Becca.

Exhaling, Becca stepped forward and reached for her hand, "Come on, I'll take you."

Becca had no choice but to get out of the water. Walking up to the beach bathroom, Becca saw a long line of swim-suit clad women and children. Joining the line, the girls sighed. It was going to be awhile.

Pulling Janessa in front of her, Becca wrapped both arms around her shoulders, trying to feel less exposed. They had nothing to do but wait and watch as the long line barely moved. All around them, they could see people with different colors of skin and silky-smooth legs. It wasn't Becca's first time to see a black person, but it was Janessa's.

They couldn't help but stare. Black people didn't live at the Crick. As far as Becca could tell, the little girls were just like them. They just had black skin.

"Heidi, Barb, don't stare. That's not polite." A woman next to the girls corrected.

And for the first time, Becca realized the little girls had been staring at them too. One of the girls pulled the woman down and whispered something in her ear, then pointed at Becca.

The line moved, and they found themselves in a large bathroom with at least a dozen toilets with no doors or stalls to separate them. Immediately Becca panicked.

How are we supposed to pee or poop? Everyone can see us?

Janessa began to whimper. Neither one of them wanted to go now, but they had no choice. It was either use the toilet or just not go. They shivered uncontrollably. Without the sunshine to warm them, their drippy clothes were almost unbearable.

At least they had each other as a door. Becca stood in front Janessa for some privacy, and Janessa did the same for Becca. The humiliation was a lot to take in as they washed up quickly and ran outside.

Becca felt so stupid for not changing into the clothes Travis had provided. Her longies were supposed to protect her, but all they did was ruin her fun. She almost wished she hadn't come, except she needed to ask Travis an important question.

Back on the beach, she wrapped in a towel and plopped down next to him. He had opened some chips and was drinking a water bottle.

Gathering all of her courage, she inhaled and blurted, "Dad, will you buy me a shaver? I don't want to have hairy legs like one of my friends."

There, she said it.

"So, you want to shave your legs, Becca?" He put a chip in his mouth and looked out to the ocean. He had to know the Mother's and Father would disapprove. Even if he tried to talk her out of it, Becca had made up her mind to find a way.

Scanning his face for any clue that would tell her what he was thinking, Becca noticed the corner of his lip curving up.

"Sure, I don't mind getting you a shaver, but I can't guarantee Mother will let you use it."

"I'll keep it put away, Mother won't see it. No one sees my legs anyways. Plus, it's not anyone's business but mine," she vowed.

"How's it going with your other mothers, Becca?"

It took her no time to find the words to vent, "Mother Susan took my soda and hid my roller blades in her closet and said she didn't know where they were..."

"...You want me to poke her in her eyeballs!" he interrupted.

"What? Dad, No."

"Poke who in the eyeballs?" Janessa had been playing in the sand quietly, but upon any news of eyeball-poking became very interested.

"You!" He said and poked her in the belly. Caught off guard, Becca and Janessa grabbed him and poked his belly. She had forgotten how good it felt to laugh with him.

9

WITH BIG CHANGES COMES BIG QUESTIONS

1997-1998

CODE OF CONDUCT: DISOBEDIENCE

Any disobedience toward the prophet should be considered as severe as death.

"I'm not sure why I have to go to high school. It's just a big, fat waste of time. What does it matter if I'm working at Levi's new restaurant instead of learning about Algebra?" Becca reasoned with Tilly as she finished braiding her hair.

Grabbing a comb to smooth any fuzzy strays, Tilly countered, "Because school is important, you don't want to grow up and be dumb! Besides, you're working way too much, and you are never home. It seems like all you want to do is work with Levi at the Golden Circle on the weekends. Once he opens up his restaurant here in town, you'll always be working with him and never be home. Boys are snakes, Becca. You don't want to get bit!"

"But Levi is like an uncle," Becca smirked at her sister's reflection in the mirror.

Tilly put the comb down, turned to look Becca square in the eye and said, "Becca, promise you won't tell anyone what I'm gonna tell you."

"Ok?" Becca promised, taken aback by her sister's grim tone.

"Levi tried to hold my hand on our drive to work last week."

"Really, that's just weird," Becca said, dismissing the thought immediately.

"It isn't weird, it's wrong, and I don't want you to be around him too much," Tilly was no-nonsense, and her protectiveness was a bit endearing, but Becca felt like she could do her own protection if need be.

"We're talkin' about me quitting school anyways. I'm not afraid of Levi. I just want to work here at the Crick and make money," Becca continued.

Tilly exhaled. "School is important Becca."

"How's it so important if the whole world is about to come to an end? You know what the prophet says. We are heading into the last days. Why does it even matter if I know how to solve math problems or know what an adjective is?"

"Becca! Seriously, hurry up! We gotta go. I have play practice this morning, and we can't be late to seminary again, I'm done talking. Stop being a brat. I'm going without you," Tilly picked up her bag and walked out the door.

Becca wasn't worried about being late because she had transportation. Taking her time, she went downstairs, grabbed an apple from the kitchen, and then headed outside to find her bike. After adjusting her leggings and dress so they wouldn't get snagged, she took off and passed Tilly within minutes.

The Golden Circle had started selling Chester Fried chicken, and Levi had plans to open a Chester Fried of his own at the Crick after the Christmas holiday. Becca had learned everything she could about the menu, so she could help him open in January.

She prided herself on her abilities to deal with customers, build excellent sandwiches, and order ingredients from suppliers. In fact, in her mind she was better at keeping stock than Levi and was convinced he wouldn't even be able to open the restaurant without her.

Glad to be alone, she had more than just quitting school and helping Levi open a restaurant to think about. Travis had called and invited the children to come to Riverton for the Holidays. With the ever-present threat of possible world-changing events, a trip was an ongoing source of conflict.

He had told them they would go shopping and try out his new hot tub outside while it was snowing. It sounded like so much fun, but the older boys had to work, and Tilly was being Tilly.

Janessa and Justin were going, though, and she reasoned that it might be good for her to go along to help watch them. Her last time off the Crick with her dad had gone well at the beach, and she felt confident that if anything were to happen, he would try his best to get them back to safety, even though he was an apostate.

Besides, she wanted to ask him if he would get her some more razors. Funny as it seemed, those razors made her feel closer to him. He understood and had kept it between them.

Relief flooded in as she made up her mind. At least for a few weeks, she could let everything go and enjoy some time having fun away from it all.

***

Sleeping in her old house in Riverton and spending time with Justin and Janessa doing fun family things with their dad was the perfect diversion for Becca's busy mind. Sitting in a hot tub while watching the snow fall was magical and walking through the mall was a blast with all the colorful decorations and smells. It felt like one adventure after another and Becca couldn't help but admire the rush of the holidays in Riverton. She missed that part of Christmas and tried not to think about what the Prophet would say, even though it nagged at her under the surface like a twisted up longie.

On the last day, Travis gave her a hundred dollars to share with the other children at the Crick for a Christmas present. Since they didn't celebrate Christmas with a tree and tons of gifts any longer, it was an unexpected treat. Becca couldn't wait to tell them and see how they would spend it.

A few days later, she found out when Father took her siblings and her Mother to see *Alaska* at the Cinemax Theater with the Christmas money. The documentary was beautiful, and Becca was proud her family was able to enjoy it because of Travis's generosity. It was the most memorable Christmas she had experienced since she was nine years old.

After the holidays, January came quickly and with it came school and the Grand opening of Levi's restaurant at the Crick. Becca barely had time to breathe between staying up until one o'clock in the morning doing restaurant preparations and then getting up at five o'clock to help get children dressed and combed to go to school. She was exhausted.

To make matters worse, she went to St. George with Travis and got braces two days before the Grand opening. Her mouth was so sore she could hardly eat. With every part of who she was, Becca wanted to quit school and just focus on work. She knew Travis and Mother would not approve. Her best hope was to convince Father Arlen she needed to quit, and then he would convince Mother.

She waited for a moment to speak with him alone one day and then started, "Father, if I can work full time, I'll help pay even more for my braces and be home more. If I stop school, I'll help Mother more at home too because I won't have homework," she reasoned.

"Now Becca, that school is gonna hate me if I pull all my children out. Maybe working full time is just too much. Maybe you should quit that instead," he said.

Terrified he might make her quit, she recanted, "Never mind, I'll just try to do better in school."

"I will think and pray about it. You should do the same. Until then keep at school," He said.

Sighing, she surrendered, "Ok."

***

Oh, I got a note!

Becca rushed to her bed and lifted a carefully folded rectangular treasure. Sniffing in Fresh perfume, she smiled. Her big sister was bossy, but she knew how to be fancy. Leaning on her bed, she opened it and began to read.

> Dear Becca,
>
> I'm just writing you a letter to tell you how much I really do love you. I wish so bad that you and me wouldn't fight. I try to prevent them, but it never works. Well, I miss you around the house. It feels like all you ever do is work, and everyone really notices it. Your family really should be more important to you. We are the ones you are going to be with in heaven, and I am quite sure there won't be a restaurant in heaven. I truly do want to be lifted up, and I know you do too. I haven't seen you pick up a good book and read it. Uncle Warren said to read from a good book every night before you go to bed. Please do this. I yearn for you, and I pray for you. The time is so short, we don't even have a minute to waste…

Lowering the letter to her lap, Becca stopped reading. Tilly's beautifully penned note had struck a chord.

Why does it make me feel so yucky?

It was true, she hadn't been reading the good book as much, and did need to work harder to be lifted up. The time *was* short, and surely there wasn't any restaurants in heaven.

Guilt crept in along with something else she couldn't quite figure out.

Life offered so much.

Why is it that I am supposed to only think about that other stuff?

Confused, Becca put the note back on the side table where she had found it and finished getting ready for work.

Tilly was satisfied with staying home, being a sweet girl. Becca admired her resolve to follow the Prophet, but Becca's hands and mind needed a challenge. Work gave her that.

Surely, I can do both.

***

"What kinda sandwich is that? It looks like crap to me."

"I wouldn't be lettin' it out that you've seen a crap sandwich!" Becca turned and gave her cousin a hug. It was Desiree.

"What are you doin' here?" Becca asked. "It's not a weekend."

"Father decided we'd move in early. It doesn't matter if our house has paint on it or not. Besides, you're lookin' at the new boss. I'm in charge of making sure you know your stuff and let me tell you, there's some work to do," Desiree held up her finger and waved it into the air as if she was checking for wind.

"What? Levi hired you? He didn't tell me! That booger!" Becca put her hands on her hips and then squealed. It was the best thing that could have ever happened.

"When do you start?" Becca asked.

"Well, now I guess. Only you will have to show me some of your fancy sandwichy stuff."

"I thought you were the new boss?" Becca teased.

"Only when it comes to crappy sandwiches."

Dang, it's good to have Desiree back!

Having her rambunctious cousin around made all the difference in keeping her motivated, but she was tired, and every day Becca felt more and more agitated. Little things started to bug her that never bugged her before. If Tilly or Jerusha left their toothbrushes out, she would have to fight to keep sweet. If another employee didn't help enough at work, she had to hold her tongue, so she didn't let them have it. Her brain started to swirl. One minute she was happy and the next she was sad or angry.

After one especially aggravating day, she came home and decided to spend the rest of the day lying on her bed curled in a faux fur leopard bedspread. She considered talking to her mother or Tilly to see if they could help her understand her moods, but decided it was just because of lack of sleep. Her brain went back and forth trying to find solutions until she was so exhausted she fell asleep.

When Becca awoke, it was almost dark. She had slept at least an hour. Afternoon naps were rare. Her mothers must have noticed she was tired and allowed her to indulge. Dinner was probably almost ready. She needed to get downstairs.

Dinner was tasteless, and all Becca wanted to do was go back to bed. Justin, Benjamin and the other boys were acting especially rowdy, and the younger children seemed super whiney. Evening prayer was almost unbearable as she knelt. Her toes went numb and her feet felt like pins and needles, but Becca managed to keep a smile, even though she felt like smacking everyone in the room.

"Are you ok Becca? You're so quiet?" Jerusha asked as the girls walked upstairs after dinner.

"I'm just tired." Becca answered.

From the laundry room, Becca heard Mother's soft voice, "Becca, can you come and see me?"

Closing the door, she handed Becca a pocket-sized paper book, and said, "Here, I have something for you. Grandma Claudia gave it to me when I was about your age."

It was purple with a picture of a woman in a pink dress holding a red rose. It was titled, *What Women Want to Know*.

"I've noticed you've been super tired. That's normal for girls your age…"

Mother went on to explain how her body was changing and that soon, she would need to take care of herself in a different way. That her body would start doing different things. It was so embarrassing. But still, Becca *was* curious to know what women wanted to know and glanced down at the small purple book.

"Now Becca, you don't need to go showin' this book to anyone. Keep it put away. This is private only for your husband to teach you about when you get married. You don't need to share it with the other children. What the book doesn't show you, your husband will." She said the words lightheartedly, but Becca knew she was serious.

My husband will teach me? About My body! Why does he even have to know? It's none of his business!

Thoughts swirled, but Becca just smiled and said, "Yes, Mother." Too embarrassed to talk any further, she went to her room, took a shower, got in bed, and pulled her blanket over her head.

Once safe under her covers, she took out the little book and a flashlight. The first page said: Copyright 1961. Glenbrook Laboratories.

It was thirty-seven years old.

As old as her mother, it had to be important. She was thankful her mother had saved it and shared it with her, but felt odd, nonetheless, for living her whole life without even a clue that her body would do what it was doing.

How was it that my mothers, grandmothers, and sisters have been doing this and now is the first time I've ever heard about it?

***

"Where's Mother and Tilly?" Becca asked Mother Susan as she and the other sisters helped wash up after the evening meal. She hadn't seen them since getting home from work.

"Why don't you check the sewing room?" Mother Susan advised question-like and somewhat cheery. It was unlike Mother Susan to be cheery.

Hanging the dish towel on the rack, Becca decided to see what was up with the sewing room. Opening the door, she could see Mother and Tilly working feverishly with some white material.

"Whatcha makin'?" Becca wondered.

Mother looked up, startled from her concentrated efforts, and smiled. "Close the door, Becca, we have news. Father got a call. Tilly is getting married tomorrow."

Tilly is getting married? How is that even possible? The prophet knows that boys are snakes and Tilly is a girl.

It was so sudden. Not knowing how to react, she stood still. Butterflies filled her belly as it all filtered through. Her sister would be married by this time tomorrow. She would have a husband who could touch her hand and look into her eyes. He would have to explain what the purple book didn't explain. Although Becca couldn't imagine what that could be, it just seemed so weird.

Mother seeped excitement and seemed pleased, so Becca figured she should be excited too. After all, the prophet had decided, and Tilly was being placed with a man of the priesthood. It was everything she had been taught was right since she could remember, but it was all just so sudden.

"Who is it?" Becca beamed and walked to Tilly, who was working quietly in the corner.

"Wally Barlow," mother interjected before Tilly could reply. "We're blessed to be able to have the ceremony at Uncle Rulon's own home. Afterward, the reception will be held at the Mark Twain restaurant banquet room."

She was so excited, she hardly took a breath. Getting married in the prophet's own home was an honor. Becca wondered why Mother was so delighted, yet Tilly seemed so distant.

Holding the white bridal piece up, Mother said, "Here Tilly, go try it on. Let's see our sweet bride."

Taking the garment, Tilly half-smiled, said "Ok," and then went to her room to try it on.

Jerusha was standing just outside the door as Tilly walked by holding the dress. Meeting Becca's eyes, she knew in an instant what Tilly was holding and donned a giddy smile. All three girls walked upstairs to their shared bedroom, and Tilly went into their closet to dress. Mother stayed behind in the sewing room.

"Who's she marrying? When? Where's it gonna be?" Jerusha fired off questions as the two girls waited excitedly for Tilly to get dressed in the closet.

"Wally Barlow. Tomorrow. At Uncle Rulon's own home!" Becca reported.

"Tomorrow at Uncle Rulon's?" Jerusha squealed incredulously as if she had just won a prize. Their fiery enthusiasm was catching. Joining hands, they waited for Tilly to open the closet door.

When the closet opened, they were shocked to see a teary, swollen face. Doused by the grim sight before them, Becca and Jerusha's fiery enthusiasm quickly turned into genuine concern.

In between sobs, Tilly forced out words. "He has red hair and big ears. I don't want to marry him! I go to school with his sister!"

Becca wouldn't have guessed she would see her sister behave this way in a million years. Tilly was bossy, but always seemed to keep sweet. For her to declare something against the prophet's choice was just unthinkable.

Jumping forward, Jerusha placed a delicate hand on her shoulder, "Oh, Tilly you look so beautiful! You'll be the prettiest bride ever. I love what you and Mother Mary have made." Tilly stood motionless and the room filled with an uncomfortable silence.

"…And to think you get to be married at Uncle Rulon's with a reception at the banquet hall. That's something everyone hopes for. I would love to be that close to the Prophet."

Wanting to say something good, Becca struggled with a dry mouth as heat blanketed her body. It seemed like the whole world was spinning. Didn't Tilly just say she didn't want to get married? Why was Jerusha acting like she didn't?

There was a soft knock on the door and Mother entered. "Oh, my girl looks so beautiful. Wally is a good man. You two will be so happy." She reached out to smooth a stitch on the dress, looked directly into Tilly's tear-stained eyes and said, "How does it feel? Does it fit well? Should we make any adjustments?"

Tilly shook her head no, "It fits ok, I think."

"Well, then, how 'bout we get a picture of the big sisters." Mother held up the camera and the three girls put on smiles before they could even think about doing anything but. Mother hummed happily and ushered Tilly to the mirror. It was like a dream, but Becca was sure it was for real and yet wished it wasn't.

***

Less than 24 hours later, the whole family gathered at Uncle Rulon's home. Nerves overtook Becca. She could hardly sit still. Everything in her world was about to change. It was almost as if she were the one getting married.

Compassion wrapped itself around her heart as she remembered Tilly's sobs in her bed the night before. Helpless to do anything that would change the circumstances, Becca had lain still and listened as her sister's life crumbled.

It was the last night she would ever sleep in her own bed. She would never walk to school with Becca again or boss her about getting ready. Becca struggled to understand and then fell asleep thinking, *this does not feel right. This does not feel right.*

Returning her focus to the present, Becca looked on as silent tears fell from Tilly's swollen eyes. Uncle Rulon showed Wally and Tilly how to hold hands, so the wedding ceremony could be appropriately sealed for time and eternity. It was the first time Tilly had even touched Wally, and he looked at her like she was a prize at the Fourth of July festival. Embarrassed and powerless, she hesitantly obeyed, and Uncle Rulon spoke the words that held power to change generations to come.

"And now you may kiss your bride…" as Uncle Rulon said the words, Becca could feel Tilly's tension rise from across the room. Wally reached out and grabbed her like they had been childhood sweethearts and gave a very stiff bride her first kiss, smiling from ear to ear.

***

Balloons, a gigantic wedding cake, and a mountain of gifts filled the Mark Twain banquet room. Cheery well-wishers walked in commenting on how beautiful Tilly looked in her dress, and several school friends showed up to congratulate her.

It was a celebration, but Becca did not feel like celebrating.

Once the presents were opened and the cake was served, it was time for Tilly and Wally to leave. Wally grabbed her by the waist, pulled her close and kissed her in front of everyone. It was evident that Tilly didn't want to be touched, but that didn't matter. She was his now, and no longer her own.

On the short van ride home from the reception, Becca sat too tired to even speak. She listened as happy comments whirled around like flies.

"Wasn't that a pleasant reception?"

"I loved the cake."

"Did you see the quilt so and so made?"

No one mentioned how Tilly cried during the whole ceremony and hardly wanted to touch the man she had just been given to for time and eternity.

That night Becca entered the room she and Jerusha would share without Tilly. It was strangely empty. She couldn't help but wonder how her sister was doing and why no one else seemed to care. Even though Tilly always seemed permanently irritated with her, she was her sister, and Becca felt protective. Why did no one else? It made no sense at all.

***

The next day was Saturday work day. More than half the house, all the men, and boys left early to work. Becca heard a knock at the front door and was surprised to see Travis.

"Travis's here," one of Mother Susan's children ran in the side door announcing his presence.

Uneasiness whirled like a summertime sandstorm. A certain level of restlessness was always present when Travis came on scheduled visits, but news of his arrival sent shockwaves through the house as Mothers started moving around like nervous rats.

Janessa scampered outside, "Travis, Tilly got married at the prophet's very own house yesterday!"

"She what?" Travis directed towards Mother.

In her sweetest voice, Mother tried to smooth the news. "She was a beautiful bride. She married Wally Barlow."

"Mary, can I have a word with you?" Travis said it kind enough, but Becca could tell he was holding back.

Mother joined Travis outside, and Becca strained to listen.

"Mary, did she even know this man? She's only sixteen! How long did you know she was getting married? She is only 16!" Travis fired off questions one after another before Mother could even respond. Becca had never heard his voice so angry.

"Travis can you please keep your voice down," Mother appealed.

After that, Becca heard talking but could not make out the words. Travis was not happy about Tilly's marriage. He was the only person who had questioned it other than Becca. Everyone else just acted like it was the best thing ever. Once again, she couldn't help but admire him. If he had seen Tilly crying, holding Wally's hand, he would have said something.

Becca heard a car door slam and Mother came back inside and informed, "Children, you won't be going with Travis today."

Becca's heart sank and was surprised to feel tears forming. There was nothing she wanted more at that moment than to give him a big hug and tell him how much she loved him. How could it be that Travis, the apostate, was the only one who shared her frustration?

10

MORE THAN JUST CHANGE
1999

CODE OF CONDUCT: PRIESTHOOD MARRIAGE

The Lord creates the love in a priesthood marriage. The woman is appointed, and the Lord makes the love. Once they obey the prophet together, the love will grow.

What? Levi is married?

Becca stood outside the kitchen and listened to her uncle's gossip. Astonished by the news, she didn't know what to say.

Levi is married? What's her name? Do I know her?

Hoping to hear more details, she went to the cupboard to get a cup.

"Yep, heard 'bout it a few hours ago. Married a girl named Sarah…"

She wanted to hear more and could have asked, but it was late, and their conversation changed to the weather and Saturday projects. Becca had worked with Levi on Friday. He wasn't married then, and he definitely hadn't said a word about getting married. She could hardly believe her boss and friend was married just as Tilly had been.

It wasn't real until the next morning at church when she saw them sitting by each other. Neither one seemed to be over-the-moon happy. Becca noticed several people glancing, whispering and pointing at the new couple like they were a rare miracle. At one time she would have agreed. Now she just wondered how, all the sudden, Levi could be a husband.

Monday, as Becca pedaled her way to work, she wondered about how it would be working with a married Levi.

How is that even possible?

She couldn't stop thinking about the prophet's decision to suddenly place Tilly, and then Levi, in marriage. It wasn't her place to question, but just couldn't reconcile what she had seen as Tilly cried on her wedding day, and no one even seemed to bat an eyelash.

And then Levi, she wondered how he felt about his new life with a wife. Her brain felt like it was being tossed around like bread dough. She recalled the time Tilly had warned her about working too closely with him. Well, maybe now she was safe.

Safer than what? She laughed at the thought. Even the idea was funny because at least 4 of her friends including Desiree, worked with her. If they wanted to, the girls could gang up on Levi and take *him* down. She laughed out loud on her bike. The girls would never, ever do such a thing. *Well, maybe Desiree would.*

Becca wouldn't even dare say it out loud, but it was a fact. The girls outnumbered the boys. Eddie, who was twelve, was the only other boy who worked with them, and she knew him from school. If she were going to get in trouble because of a boy, it would be because of him. Secretly, she thought he was cute. He was fun to be around, but because of his age, seemed harmless. Levi was like an Uncle, and she couldn't imagine what an Uncle would do to harm her.

She parked her bike behind the shop and walked in to see him prepping a batch of chicken fingers. He turned and rushed over to share the news.

"Did you see I'm married?" he offered the fact like it was yesterday's sandwich.

Becca put on her apron, grabbed some lettuce, a chopping board, and a knife, then began to cut slices, acting like it wasn't too big a deal.

"I saw you sitting by her in church."

As they prepped, Levi hardly stopped talking about his new bride. That would have been fine if he had kind things to say, but he complained about her looks and her personality. He made fun of her, and none of it seemed funny. Becca couldn't understand how he could be so openly harsh about someone he was supposed to love. If she had a husband who talked about her like that, she would definitely give him a piece of her mind.

Becca kept busy in between Levi's complaints and tried to keep focused on finishing her short shift without saying something to him she'd regret.

"Hey Levi, remember I need to get home early to help Mother with dinner before we come back to clean." Months before, Levi had arranged with her mother to help with the night deep cleaning. That way Mother made some extra money and Becca wouldn't have to be alone late at night by herself.

"That'll be ok. It's been a slow night. Sure," he said absently as if his mind was a million miles away. Which was where Becca wished she was right then, so she took off her apron and headed for her bike. Frustrations were pedaled away as she rode home and thought about Levi's attitude.

What made him think it was ok to be a jerk about his wife?

She didn't really know Sarah, but for some reason, it just made her mad. She remembered Tilly's tears on her wedding day and how everyone ignored her heartbreak.

Had Sarah cried? Did Sarah have a choice to marry the man who was supposed to love her for all eternity? Did Sarah know how he made fun of her?

It was like Sarah was just a toy or something, and not a person. Becca had never seen this side of Levi and didn't like it one bit.

Just as the dinner dishes were being cleared, she walked into the kitchen, picked some food from the stove and nibbled. She wanted to complain about Levi being a big jerk about Sarah to her Mother but couldn't trust that she would understand. Especially after Tilly's wedding, Becca doubted her Mother would understand at all.

"Becca, you'll have to start driving soon. You wanna practice by driving us tonight?" Mother asked with a sweet smile as she walked into the kitchen.

Driving was the last thing she wanted to do. Unlike her brothers, who drove when they were fifteen, Becca had no desire to learn. After all, she had her bike.

"I'm Ok Mother," she assured.

"Awe, come on, it'll be fun. You can do it." She asserted. "Just watch me. When we get there, we can switch places, and you can do a loop around the block."

Becca took a breath, and said, "Ok, Fine."

"My Lanta, you act like it's somethin' terrible. It's not that bad," Mother insisted.

"I said I'll try," Becca agreed to do it, just so she would stop talking.

A few hours later Becca sat behind the driver's wheel that dwarfed her tiny body. It was late evening, so there were no other vehicles around. She adjusted the mirrors, then turned the key and drove the short distance without any hefty mistakes. In fact, except for some jerky braking, she was somewhat proud of her performance.

She parked, and they went inside to scrub. Once they were finished, freshly motivated by her driving experience, Becca decided to back the van up closer to the door to gather their things. Mother had gone to the restroom, so Becca decided to surprise her and ran outside to move it.

She pushed the key, checked the rearview mirror, and then turned around to check as she had seen her mother do hundreds of times. Confidently, she punched the gas and the van lurched forward, crashing into the pylon that held the roof onto the building. Shocked, Becca quickly turned the key, ran to the couch seat in the back, curled up like a baby, and cried silent tears she didn't even know existed.

Seconds later Mother scurried out of the restaurant, wiping wet hands on her dress, her face as white as fresh longies.

"Becca, Becca, are you ok?" She inquired, opening the van door.

"Where are you?" She asked, puzzled at the empty chair.

"I'm here. I never want to drive again!" She yelled, her face buried in her hands.

"Oh, Becca, it's ok. Your brothers and sister have all made their marks on this van. This one will be your bend. It's not too bad. At least you didn't hit it hard enough to cause the roof of the restaurant to fall."

How Mother could always stay so sweet was beyond understanding. Becca knew she was trying to cheer her up, but her emotions were only a tiny bit connected to the driving mistake.

"I don't want to drive," was all she could choke out.

"Ok, I'll lock up and be out in a bit," Mother comforted.

Becca stayed in the back and didn't say a word on the ride home. First Tilly got married and didn't want to, then Levi got married and talked mean about his wife, and now Becca wrecked into the pole. To top it all off, her apostate dad seemed to be the only person who even saw the injustice in it all, yet her mother was the only person in the world who could make her feel loved, no matter what.

Underneath all the happenings was a nagging understanding which was starting to grow. Tilly was about a year older than Becca. If it was possible for Tilly to be married like that, then it was unquestionably reasonable for Becca as well.

It was just too much. More than just the front of the van had been dented. She felt as if one more change would cause her whole world to collapse.

***

"Jerusha, have you seen my bike?" Becca asked as she stormed back into the kitchen after seeing her bike was not where she put it.

"No, I haven't seen it since you rode it yesterday, why?" Jerusha answered, genuinely concerned. The children were all getting ready to head out to school, and the ones who heard her stared up blankly. Everyone knew Becca's bike was off limits.

"Well I can't find it, and it's not where I put it." Becca was hotter than a ham and cheese biscuit. She had promised Travis that no one would ride it but her, and she had kept her promise. The fact that it was not in its place meant someone else had taken it.

Her first thought was that Mother Susan had let one of the other children ride it like she had with her roller blades. Mother Susan was always doing that with other things important to her, but everyone knew her bike was different. No one, not even the boys would touch her bike.

"I think I saw Mason riding it last night after you and Mother went to work," Janessa said, her green eyes twinkling like she solved a famous mystery.

"Mason Johnson? Why would he think he could ride my bike?" Becca said out loud, not expecting an answer. She was not going keep sweet about this one. He had no right to take her bike.

"I'm gonna go get it!" Becca snapped.

"Becca, if he has it, maybe Father can take you." Mother hustled into the kitchen to see what was going on.

"Mother, I'm a big girl. I'll get my bike by myself. I'm not gonna let someone get away with takin' it." Becca turned, grabbed her things, and headed out to find him.

Becca hit the dirt road as fast as her blue-jean jumper dress would allow. She wanted to hold it up and run, but that would not go over well.

Who does Mason think he is?

With every step toward his house, she could feel the tension rise.

Once there, she didn't even bother to knock on the door but walked straight into his backyard. There, turned on its side, with one wheel straight up and all crusted with mud was her bike.

Heat rose to her forehead. She clenched her fists and stomped over to it. Mason had no right to take something that wasn't even his and treat it like that. Just as she lifted the bike, he stepped out on his porch.

"You seriously think it's ok to steal my bike?" Becca yelled.

"Don't you even think about touchin' my bike again! You can't just take somethin' that doesn't belong to you and treat it like crap!"

Becca turned and walked the bike toward home without even looking at him. She couldn't ride it to school like it was. It would get her dress all dirty.

The only other time in her life she had felt such anger was when Levi had made fun of Sarah. She didn't quite understand her outrage at the time but was fully aware of it now.

"Don't even look at it!" She yelled, not even sure if he was still standing outside, and not even caring if he heard it or not. It just made her feel better to say it.

***

Father had finally given her permission to go to school half-time, so Becca was able to leave school by lunchtime. The afternoon commute was one of her favorite times of the day. Since the younger children were still in school, she was able to walk alone and bask in the noon-time sun without a lot of commotion.

Over the last few days, she had noticed an unfamiliar white suburban cruising by on the dirt road. Both times she had been riding her bike and hadn't really gotten a good view of who was driving. But because Mason had messed up her bike, she was walking and could get a better view as it passed her again.

The hairs on the back of her neck stood up. It was a boy behind the wheel. She couldn't make out his features but could tell he was looking at her.

He's driving by on purpose.

Feeling flattered, excited and nervous all at the same time, she quickened her pace. It was a new sensation, and she liked it. Even though it was utterly forbidden, she couldn't help but be curious as it disappeared in the distance.

A familiar container of warm chocolate chip cookies sat on the counter as she entered the kitchen. Curiosity bubbled in her belly as she considered the motives of suburban-boy. Grabbing three cookies and a glass of fresh cow's milk, she made her way to the balcony just off her bedroom to do homework and draw before work.

In the distance, she could see all the way to the Hildale border on the Utah side and the red rocks that made up her childhood playground. Below her balcony was the road and dirt side path she walked or rode her bike on every day.

Minutes later she heard a familiar noise, and her heart jumped like a spring-time bullfrog. The white suburban was heading toward her house. It stopped right under her window, and the engine revved. From her position, she held a clear view of the light-brown haired boy who was looking straight at her with two huge blue eyes. Head bent, he leaned out the window, half-smiled, and waved. Tilting her head the same way, she raised her hand and waved back.

If boys were snakes, he was the cutest snake she had ever seen.

Other than her silly, secret admiration of Eddie from work, Becca had no experience of being attracted to a boy and had absolutely no clue what to do with the new-found fascination. Staring at the back of the suburban, she willed it to turn around and come back. When it didn't, she fought disappointment.

Who was that and why did he want to see me?

It was almost as exciting as the first time she had ridden a bike. She was determined to find out who he was and get to the bottom of it.

A few hours later at work, while Desiree, Rachelle, and Becca fried chicken, Becca tried to do some investigating.

"Hey, do either of you know who drives a white suburban?" If she could trust anyone, then it would be Desiree and Rachelle.

"I think the Cooks have one. Why?" Desiree questioned.

"Today it went past my house really slow and kind of revved its engine a little. It was weird," Becca said.

"Trucks don't just "rev" their engines, people do," Desiree said, lifting her eyebrows playfully.

All three girls were aware of a boy's snake status but were becoming more and more curious. From the way Desiree asked the question, Becca could tell she was following.

Leaning in, she whispered, "He was cute."

Giddy, Rachelle popped in, "Oh, I think that's probably Mac Cook. He's related to me somehow."

"Oooooh, Becca has a boyfriend!" Desiree teased loud enough for Levi to hear.

"Seriously, Desiree, I don't want people to know. Besides I don't even know who he is," Becca whispered and looked to see if anyone had noticed.

"Well, maybe he's stalkin' you to get to me," Desiree laughed.

"You're so dumb," Becca laughed and then rushed to the chicken, "We better get this chicken out and get more fries cooking."

It went against everything she had ever been taught but couldn't help herself. At least for now, she knew his name. Mac. Mac Cook.

***

Some evenings Becca and the other children would lie on her Mother's bed and talk for hours. It was apparent Mother loved all the children, not just her own blood children. She had a way of listening that made them feel cherished and loved.

Secretly Becca felt great pride for the fact that her mother was the "favorite" mother. Even Mother Susan's children found their way to her bed to talk and, although she never said a word out loud about it, Becca knew Mother Susan was jealous.

One night Becca found her way to Mother's room where she was folding clothes, grabbed a towel, and sat down to help.

Once courage was mustered, Becca asked, "What if I think a boy is cute?"

Mother put down the item she was folding, looked her square in the eye and said, "Becca, are there any boys seekin' you out?"

"Oh no. I just noticed a boy the other day I've never seen before and thought he looked nice. That's all."

"Becca if a boy is seekin' you out, he is surely up to no good. Only the prophet knows what man you should be with. If you try to do it on your own, it can be very bad," She urged.

"It's not good to look at a boy and think he's cute. You have to fight those thoughts and talk with Heavenly Father," She pleaded.

"I know Mother. I know. Don't worry about it," She shrugged and picked up another towel. The room grew silent as the two folded.

Wanting to ease her guilty conscience, Becca decided to talk about the school situation.

"Mother, I spoke to Father about quitin' school altogether a while ago, and he told me to pray about it."

Mother kept folding and asked. "Well did you?"

"Well did I what?" Becca asked.

"Pray about it," Mother said.

"Yes, and I think it'd be best if I quit. If I get to work full-time it'll help with paying for my braces even more and maybe help with anything you need," Becca added the last little bit in just to keep her reasoning more thoughtful. Even though she had used the same rationale with Father, it held different weight as she related it to her mother.

Mother looked up from folding and said, "Well, I'll talk to Father. If you prayed about it and Father feels ok with it, then I think it might be ok."

"Thank you, Mother!" Becca rejoiced and jumped over to hug her. "It'll be so much better for me if I can quit."

"Well good, then. Now let's get these clothes done and get to bed." Mother ended with her ever-present smile.

"Ok," Becca answered and got to work folding.

"Becca, just remember," she paused, her smile flattened into a solemn line, "if a boy is givin' you attention, he's not a good priesthood boy."

"I know, Mother," Becca assured.

She deeply loved her Mother and did not want to disappoint her in any way but had no idea how hard it was going to be to resist the boy who was about to be "givin" her some attention.

11

THE TROUBLE WITH CURIOSITY
1999

Even though she knew it would disappoint her Mother, Becca couldn't help but think about that sandy-haired boy. When she wasn't working or doing family chores, she would ride her bike around town hoping to run into the suburban and see where he lived. Once in a while, he showed up in church, but it was hard for Becca to make out his schedule. He never seemed to be consistent.

Over the course of a few weeks, she subtly gathered little pieces of information from several different sources, trying hard not to be too conspicuous. Levi proved to be an excellent source.

"Levi I've noticed there are boys my age in church that I don't ever see at school." Becca started one afternoon as she and Levi prepped the chicken.

Levi looked up, checked the produce list, and pulled out some tomatoes.

"Well, lots of boys work out of town and don't go to school."

There it was again. Boys didn't have to go to school if they were working. That didn't seem fair. Becca had worked out of town on

Saturdays from the time she was eleven at her Uncle's restaurant, but she would never have been allowed to quit school at such a young age.

"Several fathers run different construction companies all over Arizona and Utah. The boys who are old enough go to work," he continued.

"So, they don't have to go to school ever? Even younger boys?" She pushed for more.

"Why do you care about what the boys do or don't do?" Levi looked up with suspicion.

"I don't know, I just notice things," she stated, trying to sound innocent.

She knew her interest may give Levi some concern but didn't feel too worried because Levi wasn't perfect either. After all, she had seen him flirt a little before he was married.

"How do you know all this?" She dared to push forward.

"Well, I hear things at our priesthood meetings," Levi put down his knife and focused his full attention on her. "Why're you so interested in boys all of a sudden?"

"Oh, I just wondered. That's all." Becca replied, full knowing Levi had worked with her long enough to see she had other reasons for her questions.

Realizing it was time to back off, she said, "I'm gonna go stock the sandwich area," then headed to the back.

***

Against everything Becca had ever been taught, she joined the church choir, hoping to catch his eye. She sat with the other choir girls in front of the congregation scanning familiar faces, looking for a blue-eyed, sandy-brown haired boy. Two Sundays in a row she had scanned and found his family but had not seen him, and she was getting discouraged.

Then, just like he could read her mind, he walked in and took a seat in the very back.

Look up, look up!

A crooked smile finally greeted her, and the whole room spun. She felt herself flush just as the hymn ended but confidently smoothed her purple chiffon dress, adjusted her braid, and took her seat. Becca had a perfect view of him, but hundreds of people between them had an excellent view of her.

Purposefully, she avoided looking his direction too much because she couldn't help but make a huge smile. Hoping to appear busy, she turned to her notetaking tablet.

Occasionally, she glanced his direction. Without fail, she was met with two blue eyes gazing back. He held the advantage; the people had their backs to him. No one could see his face. One time she lifted her hand to her brow and slowly looked up to find him putting his hand to his forehead. He was copying her. It was a childish game she and her siblings used to play, but it was different and exciting when it was forbidden with hundreds of church members between them.

Uncle Alvin's talk droned on and time passed unusually fast as they silently conversed. Right before the closing prayer, Becca looked up to find him with his finger by his chin, silently inviting her to do the same. Unable to hold it in, she giggled loud enough that heads around her lifted up and she quickly dropped her eyes to her notes, careful to keep her gaze down the rest of the time.

On the surface, it was just like any other Sunday. Becca went to church with her family, served the younger children the big Sunday dinner, helped with clean up, and then went upstairs for quiet time on the balcony where she had first seen him drive by. On the outside, all was normal. On the inside, every thought was centered on the crooked smile of a boy she had no business thinking about.

Calm evening air welcomed her as she stepped onto her balcony. Opening her notebook, she took a purple gel pen and began to draw flowers on the black paper as the sun retreated on the horizon. This flirting was utterly wrong and went against everything she knew to be a good, "sweet" girl. Despite what Uncle Warren had taught at the Alta Academy, she convinced herself it was innocent enough and allowed herself to play. But, the game she was playing with Mac was different. He was different.

Just the tip of the evening sun could be seen. Becca watched it slip away along with any light she could use to draw by. Disappointed a white suburban hadn't passed, she got up and stretched.

Oh well. We had fun playing.

For all she knew, he may have been making fun of her.

Two lone headlights rounded the corner just as she was about to walk inside. It was too dark to see a face, but Becca knew it was him. A strange excitement swirled inside her belly.

As suddenly as the lights showed up, they passed. Rejecting red tail lights glared at her through the dark. Frustrated, Becca fought the urge to get angry. *What did I expect?* It wasn't like he could come over and visit.

Or could he?

The two red lights stopped moving, just up the road by the Spud Pit. Becca sat down to think. He parked.

What does that mean? Is he inviting me to come and see him? He wouldn't dare. Did he get a flat? Did his truck die?

Unanswered questions filled the night air as Becca watched for any sign that he was there to see her. The strange connection she had felt earlier in church returned, pulling her toward tail lights that punctured the night horizon.

In an instant, the lights went out. Not out like they drove off, out like they were turned off. It made the darkness complete; Becca couldn't even see her hand in front of her face. Under the veil of darkness, she felt brave and decided to walk down to see if he was there for her. If he weren't, no one would even know she had dared to find out.

It wasn't hard to get out of the house without being noticed. The younger children had been put to bed at least an hour before. Father had turned in early with Mother Susan, and the other Mothers were busy in their rooms. They probably thought she was already in bed.

Sneaking out through the basement door, Becca made her way toward the Spud Pit. Unintimidated by the darkness, she confidently put one foot in front of the other. The dirt roads of the Crick were so natural to her; she could walk them blindfolded effortlessly without stumbling. As recognizable as they were, the emotion brewing in her heart was as foreign as the moon.

There was a block-like, darker shadow sitting on the road just before the pit. It was the suburban.

Now what?

It was too late to turn back. The grand confidence she had felt just minutes before melted, but curiosity and pride pushed her to seek further. With all the courage she could muster, she walked straight up to the truck and knocked. The window came down, and a shadow of a face could be seen.

"Hi," his voice broke the silence.

"Hi," she echoed.

"Wanna go for a cruise?"

"Uhh, Sure," she answered like it was an everyday decision.

She walked around to the passenger side and climbed into the suburban, careful to close the door quietly. He turned it on without the lights. Just up the road, he flipped them back on, and the two sat in silence. The cab of the suburban smelled nice, like the cologne her dad wore. Lightheaded, she digested the reality of her actions. Driving alone with a snake-boy was forbidden.

Soft country music played on the radio and the two rode in silence. He had come to see her. Just her. Becca had no idea of what to say. She had been alone with boys before, like Levi, or Eddie at work, but this was entirely different. Powerless to speak, Becca sat with her hands folded in her lap and wondered what to do next.

The silence between them spoke volumes. Both knew they were risking his priesthood by driving around together. If any adult knew what they were doing, he could even be kicked out of town.

Why would he risk something so dear?

He didn't even know her.

Occasionally, she stole a glance in his direction. The green light from the odometer and white light from the radio gave her just a faint view of his jaw. He wasn't just cute; he was exceptionally good looking. Unlike his playful faces in church, he seemed almost businesslike, and she wanted to know what he was thinking, but couldn't gather the nerve to ask.

Somehow in the sea of darkness and unspoken words, she noticed the clock on the dashboard.

"It's almost midnight," she said, breaking the silence.

Hearing her own voice brought her back to reality, and she immediately panicked at the thought her Mother could have gone into her room to check on her before she went to bed.

"We should get home," He replied.

"Yes." Becca agreed.

He turned the lights off just before the Spud Pit and stopped the suburban. Deafening silence hovered in the thick air of unspoken thoughts.

"Ok, well, I guess I'll see you around," Becca rushed to open the door.

"Ya, we can do this again sometime," He answered shyly.

With that, Becca climbed out of the truck and speed-walked the short way home. They had been together for three hours and said less than twenty words apiece, but for her, it was the most exciting thing that had ever happened.

"It's so weird," Jerusha whispered.

"I wonder why there's pink wrinkly skin under it." Becca followed.

"I don't know. I think that's where the pee comes out, but I don't get the other parts," Jerusha said.

Winston was nine months old and Mother Susan's youngest child. Jerusha and Becca were left in charge of tending him one Saturday afternoon while the other Mothers were busy. Changing a baby's diaper wasn't unusual for the girls, but in their family, they only had one little brother, and the rest were little sisters.

Courageous with each other by their side, the girls glanced at him a little longer than was necessary to change a diaper and pondered their questions out loud to each other.

Through Becca's peripheral vision, she noticed some movement to her right. It was Mother Susan. She had paused in the hallway. Hoping she hadn't seen their curiosity, they looked at each other with concern and quickly covered him.

A short time passed, and they heard over the intercom, "Becca and Jerusha please come to my room."

Mother Susan's voice was matter of fact and strangely polite. Startled, both girls jumped at the sound and stood stock still. An overwhelming feeling of shame covered them.

Becca mouthed words to Jerusha, "What did she hear?"

"I don't know," Jerusha returned.

Neither girl spoke as they made their way to Mother Susan's room. If there was one person in the world she would rather not know they were just wondering about a baby boy's parts, it would be Mother Susan.

"Close the door." Her face was solemn and her voice unfriendly.

Obeying her quickly without a word, Jerusha pushed the door shut, then they waited in silence. After a moment, Mother Susan spoke.

"I want to meet with both of you later tonight on the basement stairs after the other children have been bathed and put to bed."

"Ok." Was all they could choke out of their dry mouths.

***

Trying her best not to think of what Mother Susan would say on the stairs that night, Becca rushed back to her chores. Ashamed and afraid, she did not want to have any time around her own Mother, who always knew when something was wrong.

Thankfully, it was her turn to make the family bread that would last through the big Sunday meal. With dozens of people to feed, that was no small feat. Measuring ingredients into the big mixer, Becca had trouble keeping count of the cups of this and teaspoons of that.

Did I remember to put in the yeast? Was that the right amount of salt?

It was useless. She couldn't concentrate to save her life. It would be what it would be. They had eaten flat, tasteless, bread before. They could eat it again.

If Mother Susan wants to punish us, why doesn't she just do it?

Her thoughts ran wild as she tried to figure out any possible good outcome from meeting on the stairs. If Becca had learned anything in the last few months about Mother Susan, it was that she could not be trusted. She was mean and had her favorites, and Becca was not one of them.

The evening wore on, and the boys returned from Saturday work day. With them back the house was alive and busier. It was good to have the distraction of loading the food onto the table and helping the younger children get their plates. Just as she thought, the bread came out flat and hard. It was embarrassing to even serve it, but it would have to do for the next three meals.

"Our Heavenly Father, we thank you…" Father prayed, and Becca closed her eyes, trying to listen, but all she could hear was Mother Susan's voice coming over the intercom.

Why did we have to talk about it?

All they had to do was change his dirty diaper. Why did they have to say what they were thinking out loud? It wasn't like he was an evil boy, he was a baby.

"…And we pray that our children can make good choices to help them to keep sweet as the prophet requires…"

Peeking up, Becca looked at Father to see if he was looking in her direction.

Was he directing the prayer toward Jerusha and me? Had mother Susan told him what we were doing?

That moment she noticed that Jerusha, too, had opened one eye to see if the prayer was intended for her. Both girls saw each other and quickly closed their eyes. Becca resolved that, like the bread, it would be what it would be. She just couldn't do anything about it.

After deciding she couldn't do anything about the consequences that awaited her on the stairs and enduring the giggles over her pitiful bread, it seemed like the evening flew by. Saturday nights were the busiest nights of the week as Sunday was a day of rest. All chores needed to be done the night before; all children had to be bathed, hair washed and all. Dutifully, Becca and Jerusha performed their Saturday tasks helping with the younger children and cleaning as best they could.

When it was time, the duo walked to the basement stairs without a word. Each had already bathed and put on their night clothes. They were ready. It didn't matter what the punishment would be. Nothing could be worse than the day they had just endured.

Mother Susan was waiting on the stairs. Jerusha and Becca glanced questioningly towards each other and found a spot as Mother Susan pulled out what looked like a young child's book.

"Girls, I'm gonna teach you some things. You are old enough to know that boys are different." Using words Becca had never heard along with the child's anatomy book, she explained how Heavenly Father made boys different than girls.

She also explained that a man's sperm was what fertilized a woman's egg, and that was what made a woman pregnant.

Looking at the pictures, Becca just didn't want to imagine, though, how that sperm would get from the man to the woman. It was all just so weird, but she was too embarrassed to ask any questions.

Closing the book with a stern face, she added, "This is a very private personal thing. You don't need to be talking about it with your friends or tell the other mothers we had this talk. It's usually a husband's place to explain these things to their wives."

"Ok, we won't," Becca and Jerusha agreed.

As she often did, that night Becca laid awake thinking about the events of the day. All she could think about was sitting next to Jerusha on the barely-lit stairs learning about body parts.

Nothing could have surprised her more than what Mother Susan had shared. She wondered if Wally had explained that to Tilly. Maybe that was what Mother had referred to when she mentioned there was more than the purple book.

Becca just couldn't picture Tilly talking to Wally or doing such things. But then, before today, she would have never considered Mother Susan would do such a thing either.

And she had to have done it at least 5 times because she had 5 babies.

Becca felt sick. Whether it was from the thought or the brick-like bread from dinner, she wasn't sure.

***

Becca bundled her coat tightly as she sat and listened to Uncle Warren speak. It was early March, and snow had fallen the night before, so the church was cold. He was talking about the dreaded, Armageddon times and inevitable destruction to come. His prophecies had become so familiar, she was less sensitive to their sting.

But two things were different this time.

One thing was timing. The dreaded year 2000 was just around the corner. People had maxed out credit cards, preparing for it with stockpiled food and supplies for years. It had been prayed about and worried about off and on over the last decade.

The other thing was that Becca had not kept sweet. Late night Mac-meetings had become a regular activity. He had given her a blue flashlight which made communications more manageable, and they devised a code of communication based on flashes of blue light. It was a crude code, but it worked. Each time they met, her nerve got a little stronger, and on at least two occasions, they had even held hands.

Because of this, Becca wondered if she shouldn't pay better attention to the prophet's warnings and take them a little more seriously.

> *"...Be about your repentance so peace can be upon you. China and Russia are joined to attack this nation. We will be right in the middle of it. Turmoil will spread across the land. We must be filled with the holy ghost worthy to be lifted up to be protected..."*

Uncle Warren went on. His words were terrifying. China and Russia were going to destroy the United States. Somehow all computers would crash, and no one would be safe. This time his warning held a little more weight, and she paid more attention.

What made her even more attentive was the fact that Uncle Rulon, the prophet himself was in attendance. He had been sick for some time after a stroke and hadn't been to church. Uncle Warren had been speaking for him, but today, he stood to speak for himself. His speech was painfully slow and muffled, but it was a strong word. Becca wrote.

> *"...China and Russia are preparing to come against us to destroy us. We've got to be lifted up. Russia and China are joined to destroy North America. You will not survive unless you keep sweet. Let us all be prepared.*

Obey your priesthood head. If you are not one, you are not mine. Keep sweet no matter what. I love you."

Becca put down her silver gel pen and looked up as Uncle Neilson said the closing prayer.

I must keep sweet! Me and Mac must stop seeing each other.

After Sunday dinner and chores, Becca excused herself to her room early. She had a note to write, and it had to be done before she met Mac at the Spud Pit.

***

One. Two. Three…The blue light flashed. It was time.

Becca gathered her courage and the carefully penned note she had written earlier and slipped quietly through the house.

This will be the last time I will do this. I will keep sweet from now on, I want to be lifted up with the righteous, the only true chosen people.

She rehearsed the thought over and over with each step towards the parked truck. Instead of feeling peace, she felt a strange numbness. He was her friend. How could having a friend be so bad? How could it be that he was a snake?

It is not for me to question the prophet. It is not for me to question the prophet. It is not for me to question the prophet.

Her heart was pounding by the time she reached the shadow, and in the darkness, she could make out a face. He was sitting on the tailgate of his truck waiting. The struggle between right and wrong was right in front of her. She stopped abruptly and handed him the note.

"I can't come tonight. This will explain. We just can't do this anymore." She spoke just to fill up the uncomfortable silence of the night. Mac didn't say a word.

He never did say much, but she could tell, especially this time, he didn't know what to say. With every part of her body, she didn't want to leave and fought the urge to just get in with him. Her heart wanted to explode and rebel against her childhood teachings, but instead, she turned around and made her way back home, full knowing he was still sitting on the tailgate wondering what just happened.

The whole way home, Becca repeated to herself: *I can't question the prophet. I can't question the prophet…I can't question the prophet…*

12

THE BEST LAID PLANS
1999

CODE OF CONDUCT: STAYING WORTHY

Natural disasters and earthquakes respond to his command. Our prophet knows how to regulate the weather and any natural disaster he chooses. At his word, adversaries of our people will be controlled by him. But, this depends on our worthiness. He will not do it if we don't do our job of keeping worthy. If we are worthy, the Lord will let him know.

"We need a plan," Becca announced to Rachelle and Desiree. It had only been one week since she had given Mac the note and she needed to fill the void left in her thoughts. It would be impossible to be good if there was nothing to look forward to.

"We could do a picnic down by the reservoir," Rachelle offered.

"You always want to do that," Desiree pointed out. Unafraid to share her mind, Desiree had no problem steamrolling Rachelle.

Eager to help, Rachelle continued, "We haven't ridden horses for a while."

Uneasy with the idea, Becca cautioned, "The last time I rode a horse with my cousin, I fell off."

Desiree rolled her eyes.

Pursing her lips, Becca thought, *why does Desiree have to be such a booger?*

"You could ride one by yourself. That way you have more control," Rachelle assured.

Not wanting to crush Rachelle's idea just because of her own fear, Becca conceded. "Ok. That does sound fun, but we'll have to do it Friday. I work all week."

"This Friday is too soon to ask my Father," Rachelle said. Her father was usually the hardest one to give. Three girls going on an outing without a priesthood man present was not something to be taken lightly. The girls knew that they would need to appear especially sweet and be helpful to their Mothers as well if they wanted to do anything that offered freedom. Their fathers would naturally want to make sure their motives for such an outing were pure and safe. For the first time in a few months, Becca's motives were precisely that.

"So next Friday, then?" Becca confirmed, and they all three agreed.

***

When she was sneaking out, weekends had been a source of excitement for Becca. She loved anticipating Mac's return, but as the weekend approached, she dreaded its arrival and willed it to stay away. Often, he would drive through work to order a soda, just to catch Becca's eye from the window. He would smile, and she knew to look for the blue light later in the evening.

Friday didn't stay away, but Mac did. In fact, the whole weekend dragged by without her even seeing his truck. Fighting disappointment, Becca reminded herself that this was all for the best. The world was going to end soon, and she did not want to risk not being chosen. And worse, she didn't want Mac to lose his priesthood.

It wasn't hard to stay busy when she was trying to get her Father's approval for riding horses. With dozens of children in the house, messes and laundry were never in short supply. She had regular day-work at the restaurant, chores at home, and then back to the restaurant to clean with Mother. Any time Father was around, she made sure to have eye contact and smile sweetly.

Also, to keep her goodness visible, she volunteered to help in the church kitchen, cooking for the Saturday work crews, and then went home to prepare for Sunday. It was exhausting to keep up the appearance, but she knew if she wanted to go ride horses with the girls, it must be done.

That Sunday after family prayer, Becca decided it was time to ask permission. "Father, Rachelle, Desiree and I wanted to go horse riding, Desiree's father already said yes."

Father lifted his gray eyebrows and asked, "Who'll be with you?"

"Just us," Becca assured.

"When were you thinkin' about doin' this?" He questioned.

"Next Saturday morning after I finish work," she answered.

"Whose horses are you gonna ride?"

"Rachelle's neighbors. We'll ride 'em, and the owner said we have to shovel their stalls for letting us ride." She added the last bit hoping he would see their fun outing as some sort of service as well.

"I don't see what it would hurt…as long as your mother doesn't need you and come home right after," he said.

Becca looked at her Mother who was sitting next to him. She smiled back and nodded her approval.

"Thank you!" Becca beamed. It was a plan.

***

Saturday morning couldn't come quick enough. After returning home from Saturday morning meeting with Father and the older teenagers, all the men headed to their Saturday work project assignments. Becca ran upstairs to gather what she needed for the ride and made her way to the kitchen to grab a huge bag of cookies and a bottle of water. A few minutes later, Desiree walked through the door like she owned the place.

"Hey nerd, you ready to go ridin'?" Desiree teased.

"You're such a booger!" Becca teased back as they made their way outside.

Becca's heart fell as she recognized a familiar vehicle coming up the road. In her preoccupation with getting permission to do the horseback riding plan, she had forgotten it was Travis's weekend visit time.

"Ready to go to St. George?" Travis asked as he rolled down his window.

"I'm on my way to go ridin' horses with Desiree and Rachelle," Becca moaned.

"Becca, I just drove 4 hours to come and pick you up…" He stopped mid-sentence and looked around as if he forgot what he was saying.

"Where are Justin and Janessa?" He asked.

"They're inside. Dad, I planned this for weeks. Father has already given me permission. Can I go ridin' for a bit while you do somethin' at the Crick with Justin and Janessa?" Becca reasoned.

After considering the offer, Travis closed his eyes, took a deep breath and countered.

"Alright well, I'll come help you set up the horses, so you can make it a quick ride. I'll pick up the other kids, and we'll go have lunch until you're finished."

Irritated by the sudden change of plans, but grateful her dad had agreed, Becca scowled as they hopped into his truck and drove to the barn. Rachelle was already there waiting, brushing one of three saddled horses. Her neighbor stood, gloved hands to his hips with a suspicious stare as Travis's truck pulled to a stop.

Travis got out of the truck and held his hand out to shake the neighbor's hand. He took it without removing his glove.

"Thank you for letting the girls ride," Travis said.

"They're welcome to ride anytime," He offered, and then turned to address the girls. "Some girls took 'em out last week and rode 'em pretty hard. They may want to run, so just keep the reigns tight."

"Ok, we will," they agreed.

Each chose a horse and mounted, tucked their dresses around their jeans, and readied to ride.

"These horses seem really antsy, Becca," Travis cautioned as one of the horses shook his head nervously.

"They just want to run. It'll be ok. We'll be careful." Becca assured. She just wanted to get out as soon as she could. Guilt had started to creep in as she thought about how Travis had driven all that way to see her, but not enough to make her leave the plan altogether.

"We'll try to be back soon," Becca assured and grabbed the reigns a little more tightly.

For a moment, Becca wondered if he would tell her she couldn't go. He didn't hold the priesthood, but he was her dad, and she would obey him.

"Just be careful and hold on tight. Come back soon," he advised, and the girls took off.

Once they were several yards away, Becca looked back to see him still watching them with his hands in his pockets. She waved, and he motioned for her to hold on with both hands.

Turning her awareness to the ride, Becca inhaled the beauty of the red mountains contrasted by blue sky and exhaled the tension of her world. Once outside town limits, on the other side of the freeway, the natural beauty could not be ignored. It allowed her to let go of the uneasiness that was ever buzzing in her mind.

The more she prayed and learned to be good, the more her disconnect grew. It just didn't make sense that the bond and friendship she felt with Mac could be so awful. Why was it that Tilly should have to marry a man she barely knew? How was it that Travis was a bad dad, but he always showed them so much love?

As if the horse could read her mind, it forced her back into the present by jerking its head and pushed its weight to run. Wound up from her own tension, Becca hadn't even noticed how uncooperative her horse was acting. Travis was right, they were very antsy. She looked forward and saw that Desiree and Rachelle were struggling as well.

"Let's make 'em walk in a row instead of one in front of the other, that way they won't try to race," Desiree suggested.

"These horses are actin' weird!" Becca said. "I think we should just go back."

"You're just scared because you fell off before. We'll be fine," Desiree said.

Rachelle looked to Becca as if she agreed but said nothing.

Just a few minutes later, Desiree's horse pulled ahead, almost daring the others to chase after.

"They're acting dumb! We should just go back," Becca yelled to Desiree.

"I think we should go back too," Rachelle agreed, trying to keep composed.

But by that time, it was too late. Desiree's and Rachelle's horses took off ahead, competing to be first. Becca was able to pull her horse's reins to her side and circled around, but she watched the girls race off, wildly out of control.

What can I do? What should I do?

Wanting to do something to save her friends, she held on, confused. Her knowledge was primarily based on what she had learned from riding doubles with Lea the summer Arlinda was born. Fighting to sit up straight, she held the reins, and the horse pressed to pull ahead to run with the other horses. Just as she thought he was reined in, her horse jerked its head and took off on a full run.

Immediately she realized the speed had become dangerous. Her tiny body was no match for the mighty animal's strength, and she had no idea what to do. Grasping the reins tightly, her hands burned as the leather tugged against her skin. She wanted to readjust her grip but didn't dare risk losing her grip, so she just squeezed tighter.

Becca was about 20 yards behind the other girls and could see ahead that there was a T in the road. To make things worse, the T was paved.

Becca imagined what was going to happen before her friends could even react.

Ahead, one at a time the girl's horses tumbled at the intersection like bowling pins as the horses tried to make a sharp turn without traction on the paved road. Sickening screams ended with thuds on the pavement.

With her own reigns pulled so tightly that her horse's head was directly over her left leg, Becca held on, hoping her horse would slow and turn before it was too late. Metal struck pavement and a grinding, slipping noise that seemed to last an eternity filled the air as her horse barely made the turn and found its way to the shoulder of the road that wasn't paved.

Once it gained its footing, the frightened horse galloped back towards the barn, running away from the girls. Becca panicked thinking about the two blue crumpled heaps lying on the pavement. Determined not to leave her friends, she tried to muscle the horse one last time to slow it down, but she was no match for the powerful beast. Becca decided to make a jump for it.

Without thought of the consequences, she let go of the reins, unhooked her feet from the stirrups, and jumped backward off the galloping horse like she knew exactly what she was doing.

Hot desert dirt hit her face as she rolled to a stop. The impact had taken her breath, and she laid still, wondering if she was injured. Air entered her lungs and she turned onto her side and sat up. Weeds and debris tangled her hair and her blue dress was filled with dirt. Her jeans were torn at the knees. She wasn't bleeding, but her ears were ringing like she had shot a gun.

She stood up, uninjured, determined to check on her friends. Surprisingly, she looked up to see two hobbling figures making their way toward her. As they approached, Becca noticed Desiree was laughing.

"You jumped off that horse like a circus pro, and then rolled like a weed," she teased.

"Hey, I didn't laugh at you," Becca bantered back pulling weeds from her hair.

"Why not? I'm sure we looked like dorks too!" Desiree winced trying to fake a bow.

"You guys looked dead. I was worried, so I just jumped," Becca defended.

"Well, we aren't dead, but my arm feels like crap," Desiree said and looked down at her mangled arm. For the first time, Becca noticed it was hanging weird.

"That doesn't look right, Desiree," Becca said and then asked Rachelle, "How about you?"

"My ankle really hurts, but I'm ok," she said.

"We should head back," Becca urged, concerned about the shape of Desiree's arm, but relieved that her two friends were alive.

Holding on to one another, the three hobbled down the long road back toward the barn. With every step, Becca became keenly aware of her friend's injuries. She had been lucky to see the danger ahead and slow her horse. A little frustrated for not listening to her own judgment and Travis's warning, Becca vowed to give her intuition more weight the next time she found herself in a similar situation. Moments later, dust pooled all around them as an ambulance arrived, and two paramedics jumped out.

"How did you know to come?" Becca asked, puzzled as two blue-shirted men approached them and led them to sit on the bumper of the ambulance.

"Someone called in. Said they saw horses go down. You're lucky you aren't paralyzed or dead," the paramedic said as he shined a light into her eyes, checking for injuries.

They all took the ambulance up to the Hildale Clinic where Aunt Lydia checked out their injuries. She determined that Desiree and Rachelle needed to get x-rays at the emergency room in St. George for the possibility of broken bones. Except for some bruises and a few scrapes, Becca was fine.

Each of the girls called their parents to let them know what had happened, and within minutes Travis was by Becca's side.

Eyebrows drawn, he reached to give her a hug, "Are you ok? I saw the ambulances, and then the horses came running back without you."

"We're ok, but Desiree and Rachelle need x-rays. I need to go back to the stalls and get my bag. Can we go and get it and check on the horses?" Becca wondered.

"Sure. They're in the stalls cooling off," Travis assured as they walked to the car and drove the short distance to the barn. "The horses ran back without you all. Thank goodness you are ok. I never should've let you go ride," Travis asserted, and then they sat in silence the rest of the way.

Did that just happen? Becca felt like she was more in a dream than anything, but as she got out of the car and walked toward the sweaty animals they had just ridden, a big gash on the horse's leg told the truth.

"He must have caught his own leg with his shoe when we were skidding on the pavement," Becca reasoned.

"I'm glad it wasn't you," Travis shuddered.

Becca knew he wanted to lecture her, but he didn't. For as much as he wasn't around, he sure had a way of always being there when she needed him most.

He took her home to pack and let her Mother know about the accident before they set out for St. George. Harried from the shock of what had just happened, Becca packed quickly, hoping to talk Travis into letting her go to the emergency room in St. George so she could check on Desiree. He told her that was a good idea and agreed to stop at the hospital before checking into the hotel.

"I'm so glad you were there," Becca said, grateful for his support.

"Me too," He said.

"I wish I'd listened to you when you said not to ride," she continued.

"Me too," he agreed.

Becca wondered if Mac would find out about their accident and if he would be worried about her. It did her no good to wonder. Besides, her head hurt from her circus stunt.

She was glad to have the distraction of going to St. George. At least she could be in another world for two days, away from horses and snakes, and able to call Travis dad without feeling weird.

More and more she felt like she lived in two worlds. One world allowed her to listen to her heart but made her feel guilty, and the other world kept her dizzy with thought and afraid of her future.

13

WRONG BECOMES RIGHT AND RIGHT BECOMES WRONG
2000

CODE OF CONDUCT: BOYS AND GIRLS

If you get married outside of the prophet's appointing and approval, you will not go to the Celestial kingdom. Boys, you must come to a place where you'd rather die than touch a girl outside of marriage. This only happens with loyalty and love of the priesthood. Girls, also, must come to a place where they'd rather die than allow a boy to touch or even want to touch them. Once certain touching has happened, then it's all over.

Grandmother Verna played the piano as Becca anticipated the last dance of the night. She was careful to keep her eyes away from Mac as she waltzed with other boys. It had been three weeks since their last encounter. Respecting her wishes, he had stayed away.

When he danced with other girls, she couldn't help but feel strange. It wasn't as if he belonged to her. Their futures belonged to the Prophet's will, and Becca watched the whole community dance unfold before her eyes as never before.

What is the use of any of us dancing with each other?

All around the room parents and elders stood to watch for inappropriate behaviors. It almost seemed like a game the adults played to see who was flirting with who. Undoubtedly the purpose of the dance wasn't for them to get to know one another or to make friends with the possibility of a relationship and marriage. When she was younger, the community tradition was so much fun, but now it seemed like a cruel joke and didn't make sense at all.

Mother had discouraged her from attending. Even though Becca had not left any evidence of her wrong doings with Mac, Mother seemed to know something wasn't right and had asked her questions on several occasions. Becca's only defense was to stay busy to avoid any uncomfortable conversations. She found no pleasure in lying to her mother, so spending time at the dance was a perfect diversion.

She wanted to see Mac but was miserable to see him dance with other girls, so she stared forward and wished she had just listened to mother and stayed home. It was the last dance of the night, and she was ready to go home.

Why is everything so confusing?

A tap on her shoulder interrupted her thoughts. It was Mac. Trying to hide mixed emotions, she kept a straight face, stood up, and walked out to the dance floor. Taking the proper stance, the two danced like they were strangers.

Without looking at her eyes, Mac said, "Ride any horses lately?"

He knew. And he wondered about her. She couldn't help but feel relief from the visions of him dancing with the other girls.

"Who told you?" She said, stealing a glance at his face.

"I saw the ambulance and drove by to see who it was," he said.

"You were worried about me," Becca returned playfully.

"Just don't go off and join no circus. I heard you tumbled and rolled," he teased.

Not used to open flirting, Becca kept a straight face and looked ahead like she hardly knew him at all.

As she felt his hand on hers, she knew he was no stranger. Her attraction to him was so intense, she could barely breathe. Becca knew from his demeanor that he wanted to see her again that night. Two minutes of being next to him ruined three weeks of being good.

When the piano stopped, Mac released her hand, and they didn't even look at each other. In just a few hours, there would be three flashes of blue light, and she could be as close to him as she wanted without disapproving eyes looking on.

***

Sitting on his lap, holding his face, Becca gave no thought to keeping sweet. Under the shadow of the night, they were each other's world. It was like everything she had been taught since childhood was locked away in another place, and this was the only real world. Mac hadn't said a thing about the note she had given him, and she didn't bring it up.

"Why do you think we have dances?" Becca wondered aloud.

"I don't know. We just always do," he answered.

"But if boys are snakes as Uncle Warren says, then why do we get to dance and touch a boy's hand then?" She said, holding his hand.

He hesitated, then answered, "I don't think it has always been like this."

"The Prophet has always been the one to say who could marry who," Becca said.

"Well, yes, but I don't think boys have always been called snakes."

Becca thought about that. She remembered Uncle Warren saying it all the time at the Alta Academy to the girls. Mac had grown up at the Crick and had gone to public schools for his first few years until he started to be home-schooled by his Mothers when he went to work. He didn't have the same early education as she did at the Alta Academy.

"You mean you weren't told you were snakes?" Becca questioned.

"Well, we were told to leave girls alone, but we weren't actually called snakes a lot to our faces. That seems like more of a new thing," he said.

"Oh, it's not new. It's been around a long time. Uncle Warren told us all about it at the Alta Academy," she insisted.

"Well, I'll show you something he didn't tell you about at the academy," Mac grinned and kissed her.

It wasn't until later that night when she found herself in her bed just before dawn that she withdrew from the hypnotic trance of his touch. It felt odd to be that close to someone and then just leave them, but they both knew what had to happen.

She would go home and act like everything was still the same. He would go out of town and work like everything was still the same. But nothing would ever be the same.

Sneaking out with Mac became a weekly ritual. On the nights he was in town, Becca knew to watch for a blue flashing code. If she didn't see the flashes on Friday, then she was sure to count on them for Saturday or Sunday. Careful attention had to be paid to where everyone was sleeping. Although Father and her Mothers had no reason to be suspicious, Becca would take precautions to appear especially sweet. If Father Arlen were in Mother Susan's room, Becca would be extra careful walking out because there was a creaky floor panel that could arouse suspicion.

Most nights Mac would park by the Pit after ten. Becca would sneak her way out through the basement door and then walk to his truck. They were risking his priesthood, and they both knew it. But as the days and weeks passed without any of the dreaded year 2000 prophecies coming true, she became bolder even though the consequences weighed heavy on her heart.

***

Becca signed the back of her paycheck and waited for cash from the mercantile clerk who dissected her with suspicious eyes. It was expected that all children would give their checks directly to their fathers. After bills were paid, fathers would then redistribute money back to the children like an allowance.

Becca had made a deal with Travis to pay for half of her braces each month, and she had arranged with Father Arlen that she would cash her check, give money to Travis, and then give Father the rest. Rarely did Father follow up to check and see how much was left, so Becca got away with having extra cash.

She had been saving up to buy a pager. Mac had both a cell phone and a pager. The blue flashlight had worked so far, but a pager would allow them then to find each other much easier without guessing games. Buying one wasn't the problem; it was convincing Mother and Father of the necessity.

Several subtle conversations had taken place during the past few weeks over the helpfulness of having a pager. She bragged about how it could help her parents to communicate with her, and by the time she had saved up enough money to buy one, they were all for it.

Eagar to play with the gadget, Becca rode her bike over to the Radio store to buy it. Mac would be in town soon, and she wanted to try it out. In no time at all, an apprehensive salesman helped her, and she chose a sweet light-pink pager with silver trim attached to a key-chain ring. Proudly, she hooked it to her jumper dress and headed home.

They would have to create some kind of code to communicate without her parents knowing what was going on. That wouldn't be too hard. She had already thought about how it would work. The dial phone in her mother's room had the code…1 would be abc, 2 def, 3 ghi…and so on. Her number would be 25, a combination of her initials. Mac's would be 64.

Wanting to assure her mother and father that her intentions for the pager were pure, Becca rehearsed how she could explain its value. Mother Susan was the first to see it as Becca walked into the kitchen. Ignoring an icy stare and open mouth, Becca walked past her and spoke to her mother.

"Mother, look what I got today. Now you will be able to contact me whenever you need help."

"Oh, it's really cute. I'm glad it makes you happy. Now you're gonna to have to show me how to use it. So, if I want you, I can page you and tell you to get your fanny back home." She said playfully. Mother Susan, as always, wasn't amused.

If only Mother Susan knew. If only.

***

"Levi, I need to help mother with Arlinda today, so I'll be in late," Becca lied, looking down at her pager and the message it held. Mac was in town and wanted to meet up with her by the reservoir.

"Ok, well just be sure to be in before the dinner rush," Levi answered.

"I will," she said, hanging up the phone and erasing the message.

Becca's secret use of the pager had opened a whole different world. A new level of freedom to see Mac had unfolded. Before the pager, she had relied on night-time visits based on a flashing blue light. With the pager, messages could be sent any time a phone was near. As long as they picked a spot where no one could see them, Becca and Mac could see each other for short moments even during the day. Mostly it was just to wave from across the street. On rare occasions, she would even walk up beside his truck to talk.

Determined to keep her promise to Levi and get to work before the dinner rush, Becca hopped on her bike and headed out towards the path by the reservoir. After what seemed like an hour, she pulled off the side of the road and hid her bike in the bushes.

Hiking the short path up through the trees, she waited. Before too long, there was a crackling in the bushes, and she looked up to see him. He didn't look happy.

"We can't meet up. Someone's following me. I don't want to get you in trouble," Mac blurted, surveying the path.

"What? Ok. Bye."

Mac was already down the path before she had time to react.

At once she felt vulnerable and exposed. If someone was following him, they could still be around. Crouching behind a creosote bush, she waited. Quails called in the distance. The sun would be down soon. Meeting alone during the day, even if it was just to say "hi" was a considerable risk.

Why did we think this was ok? Why did we try during the day?

Her heart beat hard in her chest and she imagined the trouble he could be in. If he was to lose his priesthood, she might never see him again.

Once enough time had passed with no one showing up, she rushed down the path to find her bike and get to work. The dinner rush would be happening soon, and Levi would be wondering where she was.

Gathering her nerve, Becca stepped off her bike and straightened her dress as she walked into the building. Upon entering, she felt like everyone was watching her. Levi seemed distant and short. She had kept her promise to be there before the rush and couldn't understand his impatience.

Before her shift was over, she heard the familiar sound of Mac's truck in the drive-thru. Careful not to be discovered, she let Levi take his order and tended the front. Relief flooded in as she looked up to see his face through the window. Driving past, he held his thumb up. He had not been caught and was checking in to see if she was ok. Turning her gaze away from Mac, Becca noticed Levi staring in her direction. He saw the whole thing.

Ignoring his face, she kept herself busy and tried to calm the sudden feeling of dread that was forming in her belly.

Levi knew.

***

"Becca, bring me your pager," Father Arlen's eyes were kind, but his voice was not. Mother sat on her chair next to her bed, hands folded, and eyes lowered.

"Why do you need my pager?" Becca mumbled, unnerved at the thought of them knowing its real purpose.

"We have been given reason to believe you have been using it to meet up with a boy," Mother trembled.

Becca sat down, trying to think if she should deny the accusation or tell the truth.

"This is serious, Becca. It is not somethin' to be taken lightly. Everything we do to uphold the priesthood is not just for ourselves. It's for the Prophet and generations to come."

Their words were as heavy as bricks. They weren't sharing anything she hadn't considered hundreds of times.

"I'll go get it," Becca said, denying nothing, yet admitting nothing.

She left the room slowly but gathered speed as she grabbed the pager, careful to erase the messages quickly. Then she dashed back only to slow down before entering the room and then handed it over to Father.

He slumped as he checked the cleared memory. Without proof, they couldn't be sure of her guilt, and Mac was safe.

"Are we done?" Becca wanted to leave. She despised disappointing her mother, and it was painful to see her so upset.

"No, we're not done. I've told Levi you'll no longer work at the restaurant."

"What, Why?"

"It has come to our attention that you may be using the time away from home for other reasons than work," Father talked like he had rehearsed it in front of a mirror.

"Mother?" She turned to her Mother.

"Yes, Becca, I'm afraid so. It's for your own good. Father and I take no joy from keepin' you from somethin' you love so much, but we know what's best to keep you safe."

Becca closed her eyes and started to walk out of the room.

"Think of the Prophet, Becca, think of what he would want us to do."

Without looking back or saying a word, she gently closed the door, walked to her own room and then laid down to go to bed fully clothed.

Would the prophet approve of that? Would he be disappointed if I didn't wash my face or get ready for bed? Do I have to ask the prophet if I need to go to the bathroom?

As wrong as her thoughts were, she let them go and didn't hold back. For the first time since she was twelve, she had no job.

***

Eyes sealed, Becca turned over in her warm bed, sat up and put her feet on the ground. She stood and took one step, and then another, drifting toward the bathroom sink. She was on autopilot. Anything else required way too much energy.

The absence of a job had left her hallow, and without her pager, she had no way to contact Mac. Left with only her thoughts, she was in a dark place. Unsealing her lids, she stared blank-eyed into the mirror.

If it wasn't that Mother needed her help, she would just stay in bed all day. Despite everything that had happened, she loved her mother very much and wanted to help. So she dressed, braided her hair, and made her way toward the kitchen.

Two 40-lb boxes of tomatoes sat on the kitchen counter. It was bottling day. Becca grabbed a quick bowl of corn mush and some toast.

"Good morning Becca," Mother greeted her as she filled a huge pot with water at the sink.

"Good morning Mother," Becca echoed as she sat down to eat.

Morning breakfast had been over for at least thirty minutes. Without much of an appetite, Becca spooned the yellow, almost tasteless mush into her mouth and swallowed a few bites before getting up to help.

Mother Susan glared at Becca as she helped Mother carry the pot from the sink to the stove. Just to make Mother Susan squirm, Becca lifted her eyebrows and sweetly said, "Good morning Mother Susan."

"Not much morning left," Mother Susan murmured under her breath, just loud enough for Becca to hear as she passed by the table to get another pot.

Becca wondered how much Mother Susan knew. The whole exchange between Father Arlen and Mother had taken place in private, in her Mother's room. It didn't matter, Becca knew Mother Susan didn't seem to think too highly of her anyway. And anyone who knew Becca would notice sooner or later she was no longer wearing a pager.

All four burners on the stove were busy with huge pots that were bigger than the kitchen sink. Mother Susan tended the pots, placing tomatoes in just long enough to see the skins crack, then Mother and Mother Claudia peeled the tomatoes. Girls who weren't tending babies filled bottles with peeled tomatoes.

Boys took stuffed bottles outside, placed them in another massive pot of boiling water on the fire, stoked the fire, and then pulled the jars out when they were done. It usually took the whole day to process 80 pounds of tomatoes, even with everyone helping. It was a hot, sticky job in the heat of the summer.

As the day wore on, Becca found it hard to maintain her anger as her mother used every opportunity to say how much her help was appreciated. Becca held no pleasure in keeping secrets from her sweet mother and genuinely wanted to help lighten her load.

For a moment, Becca felt guilty as she noticed two aging hands that never held still. Even when Mother was exhausted, she always wore a smile, unlike Mother Susan who looked to find something wrong about everything she did.

Just thinking about Mother Susan brought back the anger that had started to soften. To make things worse, through the window in the kitchen, she could see a white suburban driving past. It was Mac, and there was no way she could tell him what was going on. He might as well be a thousand miles away.

"Your brows are going to stay that way if you hold it too long, Becca," Mother reminded as she noticed Becca's scowl.

Becca lifted her brows and smiled a cheesy grin, "Is this better."

Touching her shoulder, Mother said, "Come talk to me tonight when I fold clothes."

"Ok," Becca answered, and her Mother went to do some other chores. She looked at the window to see if Mac was still lingering, but he was long gone.

Dozens of quarts of bottled tomatoes lined the counter before the day was done. All Becca wanted was to go take a shower and go to bed, but she knew her Mother was waiting, so she made her way up to the room and sank onto her bed to help fold the never-ending mountain of laundry.

"You seem angry Becca, have you been seeking answers and asking Heavenly Father for help?" Mother started.

Shaking her head, Becca reached for a pair of longies and began to fold.

"I just want to work mother. Work was all I had that was all mine," Becca said. It was a half-truth, but at least it was the truth.

"I know you can find peace in this work, Becca. You just need to keep sweet and ask Heavenly Father when you don't get what you think you need," Mother encouraged.

This work. This work. At least a thousand times in her life Becca had heard the same advice. And each time the words were uttered, she had mixed thoughts and emotions.

She wanted to be sweet and wanted to do the prophet's will, but the uneasiness that was growing inside her heart would not give her peace. *This work* meant she would be unable to make her own decisions for the rest of her life. It was hard for her to imagine a loving heavenly father who would demand that.

But still, she feared the consequences of not doing what her religion required. She would be an apostate, unworthy of the prophet's blessings…worse, she would be a part of the evil outside of the Crick, and risk never seeing her family again.

"Why can't I believe in this religion and still make my own choices?"

"It doesn't work that way, Becca. We have to be obedient and trust that the prophet knows what's best. When we do that, our lives will be blessed."

"I like making my own decisions," Becca countered.

"You must pray against that urge, Becca, and trust that Father and our prophet will direct you."

Her words gave Becca no comfort at all. She grabbed more clothes and kept folding.

Mother sighed, then said, "Father has given his blessing to allow you to work at ALCO with Jerusha. Several good girls work there, and we think it would be a good place for you. Father would check on you once in a while…"

Dropping the clothes, Becca rushed to her mother's side and interrupted, "When can I start? I'll work hard, Mother. This'll be so good for me."

A genuine smile crossed her mother's face as she said, "Father has arranged for you to start next week."

"Next week!"

"Yes, but you won't get your pager back. That's forbidden. You can gain our trust back by workin' hard and keepin' up with your prayers."

"I will. This'll be so good for me. Desiree just got a job there! Can I call her and tell her?"

"I suppose," Mother returned, "But only after you help me finish folding."

Unable to control her excitement, Becca squealed and lunged forward to kiss her mother on the cheek. "I'll do better. You'll see."

14

PATH OF LEAST RESISTANCE: THE END OF THE WORLD, AGAIN

2001

CODE OF CONDUCT: PURITY

You girls are the most special girls on earth. Always protect yourselves from being soiled.

"Desiree, it's on," Becca yelled from her table without concern of being caught.

Jerusha tapped Desiree on the shoulder and motioned toward Becca. She looked up, and Becca pointed to her headphone and mouthed, "It's on."

Grabbing her headphones, Desiree found their favorite radio station and then gave Becca a confirming nod. Suspicious eyes from around the room glanced up, but no one said a word. While the other girls, including her younger sister, Jerusha, listened to homemade music from a shared music player in the middle of the table, Becca and Desiree listened to the radio on their Walkmans.

Her new job was assembling lanyards for screen printing. Girls stood around tall tables and loaded cloth pieces onto wooden jigs. It was repetitive, tedious work, but with Desiree and her Walkman, it provided the freedom Becca so desperately craved. She was paid by the number of jigs loaded, so moving fast was a good thing, and good music from the radio made that happen.

As another one of their favorite songs came on, Becca looked up to nod at Desiree who was motioning toward the door. Father had just walked in. Becca turned her Walkman off and slammed headphones to the table. Jerusha, who was working next to Becca, jumped.

Seconds later, Father waved in her direction, checking in. He had popped in regularly at first, but as the weeks had passed, he showed up less and less. Becca was earning back their trust. At her new job the only bad thing she could do was secretly listen to the radio, and that wasn't too bad.

She waved back, and he seemed satisfied, giving her a thumb up, and she knew he would be back in a few hours to take them home. Jerusha smiled reassuringly at her Father. She was such a sweet sister who never wanted any sort of conflict. Becca wished she could be more like her, and gave her a thumb up, just like Father. Jerusha beamed and got back to work.

A couple of hours later with her eyes fixed on trucks and vans passing by, Becca strained to see any sign of Mac's truck as Father drove them home. Mac had been out of town three weekends in a row. It was just as well. Sneaking out would be way too big of a risk with her parent's heightened awareness.

Becca had decided to use her energy toward spending time with friends anyway. She had asked Father several days before if she could climb up the mountainside and cook breakfast over a fire with Desiree and Rachelle. She had assured him they would walk to work together right after eating. He hadn't said no right away, so that was a good sign. It was his turn to be in her Mother's room that night, so she decided to ask him again after everyone was settled in that evening.

Becca stopped in front of the room a few hours later and heard someone talking just beyond the door.

"I'm so embarrassed," Tilly sobbed.

"Oh, Tilly, it's natural to be embarrassed, but this is a natural thing. By your second, you will be a pro."

"But I'm going to get so fat, and I feel nauseous all the time. Can I stay here tonight?" Tilly pushed the words out, and Becca felt the familiar pang of pity for her sister.

She wished she could walk right into that room, take her arm and say, "Let her stay here if she wants to," and then bring her right back into their once-shared room.

But Becca knew better. That wouldn't help Tilly. It would only serve to get herself into trouble, and with a plan looming for hiking, she wouldn't dare. So, she went back to her own room and waited until after Tilly left.

Once she felt it was safe, she knocked on the door and entered to find her mother and father sitting in their chairs reading scriptures.

"I'm just wonderin' if you and Mother had a chance to decide if I can go hike up the mountain and cook breakfast with my friends?" She began.

Father put his scriptures down and said, "Have you been doing what your mother asks and reading your scriptures?"

"Yes," she assured.

"Can you promise me that it will only be you three girls, and you will go exactly where you say you are going, and do exactly what you say you are doing?" He questioned.

"Yes, none of us want to get in trouble. We just want to do somethin' fun with each other."

Father Arlen looked to Mother who nodded and said, "We want to trust you Becca, and don't want you to be miserable. You've shown us you can be trusted going to work, now we'll allow you to do this, but you need to know, if we find out you didn't do what you said or boys show up, you won't be able to do anything with your friends for a long time."

"I promise," she beamed, grateful for their trust. Without a doubt, she missed freedom and friends and didn't want to mess that up. Despite her meet-ups with Mac, she desired to please her Mother and Father and did not want to do anything that would hinder her from her time with friends and cousins.

"Next week, then, you can go."

Grateful for permission, Becca beamed, "Thank you so much. We'll be good. Just me, Desiree and Rachelle."

She started to leave, and, despite her better judgment, asked, "Why was Tilly crying?"

Father and Mother looked up at the same time and looked at each other as if searching for what to say.

"She was just having a hard day, that's all," Mother was the first to speak, and Father seemed satisfied with the result.

"Oh, ok, I just wondered." She said and started to walk out, then paused to ask another question. "Why did she say she was going to get fat?"

"Oh, well she is going to have a baby, but isn't too far along, so she didn't want to tell everyone yet," Mother said with bright eyes.

"A baby. Tilly is going to have a baby?" Becca could hardly believe it.

"Yes, you are going to be an aunt," Mother beamed.

Becca was happy. A baby was a good reason for anyone to be happy. But Tilly didn't sound pleased, and she was embarrassed. As Becca laid in bed that night trying to figure out why Tilly would feel that way, it clicked. She remembered the talk on the stairs with Mother Susan and felt immediately embarrassed for her sister.

Wally had explained what wasn't in the purple book.

***

Pushing the last few steps up the mountain, Becca wondered whose idea it was to fry potatoes for breakfast.

"I'm glad we're here. This skillet is heavy!" She said.

"Stop whining, next time you can carry the potatoes and me too," Desiree teased.

"You are a brat, but I still love you," Becca countered.

Rachelle rolled her eyes playfully, and the three girls started to gather wood to build a fire. The horizon had just begun to shift from gray to pink, and Becca was delighted to have friends who knew how to have this kind of fun.

It had been a pain to get up at 4 am, and even more of a pain to get all three of their fathers to give permission, but now the girls happily cut potatoes and shared sweet contentment in the freedom of a new day on top of the small mountain overlooking their community.

"Wouldn't it be cool if we could hike up here with Mac and Bundle and share it with them without getting in trouble?" Becca said.

"In your dreams," Desiree said.

It had only been a couple of weeks since Becca had learned that Desiree was secretly meeting with a boy, and Rachelle had been flirting with one. None of them shared details of their flirting, but it didn't matter how deep the connections were with the boys. Just being in their presence unattended would be enough.

"Well, if we were married we could. Wouldn't that be fun if we were married and lived next door to each other?" Becca said.

Rachelle and Desiree giggled at Becca's ridiculous idea.

"What? You said I could dream," Becca countered.

Bacon crackled as they grated potatoes and broke eggs. Becca knew her boldness in verbalizing her dream was risky, but she also knew her friends, and truth be told, they wanted the same things she did. It wasn't their place to make that decision though.

And who even knew if the world was going to be around after a few months anyway? Uncle Warren's prophecies had increased again about the world's ending and mass suffering as the year 2000 approached. Becca quickly washed the thought away. Now just wasn't the time to think of reality.

Rachelle poured orange juice into three paper cups and said, "Cheers to the beautiful sunrise." The girls raised their cups.

"Cheers to friends and potatoes."

"Cheers to Desiree carryin' down the skillet."

"Cheers to Becca being a brat."

"That's what makes me, me," Becca followed, and the girls got busy eating. Ashes blew in the light breeze, and they enjoyed a brief moment of silence.

"Last week Tilly came by and wanted to stay at our house," Becca confided between bites.

"Like have a sleepover?" Desiree asked.

"Nope, she was feeling nauseous. She's gonna have a baby," Becca said as she threw her paper cup into the fire.

"What? Oh my gosh, you're gonna be an aunt!"

"Wow! A baby. That's so cool!"

Their enthusiasm was genuine and even made Becca a bit excited too.

"Having a baby is the fun part of being married. All I know is I wouldn't like to sleep next to someone I didn't know," Rachelle said.

"But you would do it if you had to," Becca reminded.

"What's all this talk of? We're here to have fun," Desiree said, waving her arm over the food and the fire.

Desiree always knew how to bring things back around, but an uneasy silence formed as the three girls watched the flames. Rachelle threw her empty cup into the fire and stared with Becca.

Knowing about her friend's secrets emboldened Becca to open up, but only cautiously. At any time either one of them could go through a righteous-streak and tell on her. The consequences of their risky behaviors were as real as the flames burning Rachelle's empty cup.

"Don't you just love seeing that sunrise?" Rachelle joined Desiree in the topic shift.

"Oh, and rainbows and sunsets too?" Desiree teased. Rachelle was always dreaming of something natury, and Becca loved it. She was innocent like that.

"Yes, it reminds me of a time we went hiking in the Grand Canyon with Father Arlen," Becca reminisced.

"Was it fun?" Rachelle asked, genuinely curious.

"Ya, but Tilly was moody because she didn't bring enough water, and Ted threw up because he ate a whole bag of marshmallows for breakfast."

"Sounds like a hoot," Desiree teased.

Becca laughed as she remembered being so proud of herself for getting through the morning hike that had seemed so troublesome at the time. Unable to relate the whole story in a way that could give it the weight it deserved, Becca said, "It was a hoot for sure."

***

"Amen and Amen to what he just delivered to me."

Uncle Warren spoke, and Becca wrote.

> *"Armageddon is very near. We must be lifted up to avoid what is soon near. We are good, but we are not good enough. Everywhere I see weakness says the Lord. If we are to be lifted up, we must prepare and judge the wicked among us. Soon the earth will be as in the days of Noah. Waters will fill this land, and the only way to be delivered is to be lifted up."*

Becca shivered at the words. In the last few weeks, she had learned of several boys who had lost the priesthood, been declared apostates, and kicked out of town. It was a scary time to be alive. Uncle Warren continued to speak, and Becca struggled to hear the ominous words in light her own choices. By every count, she would be one of the people left behind. Confused, his words made her dizzy, and she noticed she had been holding her breath.

Often, when she heard of end times, she thought about her dad, who would undoubtedly be classified as someone who would not be lifted up. It made her sad to think he would be left behind. Despite whatever happened to cause the prophet to declare him an apostate, he had shown Becca and her brothers and sisters great love, even when they were not kind to him. That had to be worth something.

She wanted desperately to talk openly with her dad about the questions she was beginning to have about her future. But that was a door she was not ready to open. He was an apostate, after all, and could not even begin to understand.

Inhaling slowly, she looked up and noticed Mac across the aisle. He had not been back to the Crick for at least a month. Just seeing him gave her butterflies. He was back. A part of her had started to wonder if he had been kicked out like the other boys.

She was so relieved there had not been evidence on the pager of her meetings with him because that would have been enough for the prophet to kick him out. His friendship was so valuable to her. Despite anything the prophet had taught, he was still one of her best friends.

He raised his brow which meant he was still interested to see her. With that signal, she knew she would find him that evening. She smiled and looked away quickly, so no one would notice their interaction.

She was determined to figure out a way to reconcile her connection to Mac with the reality of the expectations set before her by the Prophet. She did not want to be left behind. She did not want Mac to be kicked out.

There must be another way. I will pray and ask to find another way.

She reasoned with herself as Uncle Warren continued to speak of doom and destruction, all the while knowing that later that night she would be doing the exact thing she should not be doing.

"I got you somethin'," Mac smiled and handed Becca a small package.

"It's a pager!" she exclaimed as she pulled the small, pink gadget out of the box. It had a clip that made it more versatile than her other pager. "I thought that might be easier to hide," Mac said.

"I can clip it here," Becca pointed to her side under her arm. Mac looked at where she pointed and smiled. She was thinking of attaching it to her bra.

"I can help you hide it if you want," Mac offered with a smile.

"Uhhhh, I can do that myself, thank you very much!" Becca flirted.

It was just hours after she had heard Uncle Warren speak, and she knew better.

"I'll put it on silent, and you call so we can hear how loud it is," she said, placing it under her arm.

Mac dialed the number on his cell phone, and they waited in silence, and then jumped as the gadget vibrated.

"That's not too loud," she said, laughing at their jumpiness. Looking down to see what he had written. 968 6253 76453 64(you make me smile 64), 487 5878 63 64 (it's just me 64).

"It's just me." Those three words. Their existence could change the course of her life.

"Just don't ever stand too close to your parents and we will be ok," he joked.

"You should only call when I am at work or before family prayer," she cautioned.

"I'll try," he promised.

Except for the presence of the new pager, there was nothing extraordinarily different about their night together. But something was very different. If she were caught with the small device, there would be no way to explain it away.

***

Bzzzt. Bzzzt. The pager had gone off twice. It was Friday. Mac would be in town. Jerusha looked up the second time it buzzed, but Becca ignored it and kept on working loading the jig like nothing had happened. She didn't need to check it yet.

Headphones to her ears, she listened to the radio, and her hands flew as she loaded one jig after another. Her last paycheck had been a big one, and she Rachelle and Desiree had bought new, matching pajamas with her allowance. Freshly motivated by being able to spend some money, she worked harder to load as many as she could.

On a bathroom break, she asked Desiree, "Desiree, did you hear my pager go off?"

"No, but I was listenin' to my tunes," she answered.

"Do you think Jerusha could hear it?" Becca wondered.

"Well, I've heard it before, but only because I know about it," Desiree said, poking at the hidden pager.

"I don't think Jerusha would say anything anyways. She's not a tattler," Becca reasoned.

"Ya, you're probably right," Desiree agreed, and put her headphones back on and left the break area.

Becca looked down to transfer the numbers into a small notebook, 23 46 8696 2 6483 64 be in town 2 nite 64, 9268 2 6338 want 2 meet 64.

Mac was in town and wanted to meet up. She typed in the code confirming she could do it and then erased both messages. She floated back to the work area and forgot all about her previous fears concerning Jerusha and the pager.

***

Kneeling on the floor in the living room, the whole family dipped their heads, and Father began to pray. It was after 7. Usually, their family prayer was over by then, but Father had talked a little longer than usual about the prophet's words in church, their responsibilities to one another, and saying their prayers to be obedient.

Becca grew more and more anxious. Father spoke long, windy prayers that mimicked the same words he said every night. He sounded very professional with his Thee's and Thou's. On any other night, she wouldn't have even noticed, but the length of the prayer was making her sweat. She had forgotten to turn the pager off and knew Mac would probably check in soon.

Bzzzt. Bzzzt. She pretended to have a coughing fit to the rhythm of the buzz, then cleared her throat. All three Mothers and Father kept their heads bowed to finish up the prayer, but she noticed some peeking and squinting from siblings. Mother Susan glared at her when it was over. Standing to her feet, she rushed to get a drink of water.

That was close. I must remember to turn it off.

No one approached her, so she felt safe and went about her nightly chores.

One by one, siblings and Mothers made their way to bed. Becca acted like she was doing homework downstairs, so she could watch where everyone was sleeping. Except for one family member, the whole house was tucked in and quiet. In the living room, Father put another log into the fireplace and sat in his big chair reading scriptures.

Once she felt quite safe he was there to stay for a bit, she stole away to the phone in the kitchen to respond to Mac's page. There was no way she could risk sneaking out with Father still awake. Weary from waiting, she decided to join him in the living room. Blanket in hand, she walked in and snuggled down right in front of the fire.

"It's cold," Becca explained.

"Yep, it's going to be really cold tonight. Might even snow," Father said without looking up from his scriptures.

He didn't seem the least suspicious, so she snuggled in and relaxed, waiting for the opportunity to leave. Pretending to be asleep, she snuggled down and closed her eyes. About 30 minutes later, he got up and went to bed.

She waited about 20 more minutes and then, eager to get to Mac, stepped out of the blanket and slipped out the side door. Fierce, cold wind hit her pajama-clad body. She had not prepared for such cold but could not risk going back in to get a coat as she had no idea of where Father was sleeping.

Arms tucked close, she ran to the Spud Pit where Mac had been waiting.

"Why aren't you wearing a coat?" He scolded.

"Because I was pretending to sleep in the living room in front of the fire with Father. I couldn't sleep in my coat right in front of him," she answered through chattering teeth.

"Those can't be too warm either," he said pointing to her pajamas.

Becca smiled. Her pajamas were purple with little green frog princes printed all over, and they were pants. During the day she would never be seen in such clothing in public. She had bought them to match her friends, but also took great joy knowing they would share the secret of her Mac-nights.

To keep warm, Becca snuggled next to him, comforted by his body heat and the country music playing over the radio. It felt natural to be there with him, and she laughed to herself, remembering the awkwardness of their first drive together. When they were far enough away, Mac stopped the truck, and they cuddled some more and then, unexpectedly, fell asleep.

"Mac, wake up!" Becca pushed his shoulder, and he awoke startled.

"Mac, we fell asleep. It's 4:30. Holy crap! I can't believe it's morning. Father Arlen is always up by 5!" Panicking at the idea of being caught, Becca began to shake.

Mac jumped and started the truck. It had snowed, and the dirt roads were hard to make out, but he floored the gas and made it to the Spud Pit in record time.

"I can get you closer. It's so cold out there," Mac said.

"No. I'll figure it out," Becca said, jumped out of the truck, and ran toward her home barely even feeling the cold.

From outside, she saw Father through the window sitting in the same chair next to the fire where he had sat the night before. Frantic, she tried three locked doors until realizing her only choice was going to be to walk through the front door and pretend she had gone for a morning walk. A chill settled into her body as she looked down to see her new slippers were dirty and soaked from the snow.

That was the least of her worries.

15

GETTING CAUGHT AND CANADA
2002

CODE OF CONDUCT: MARRIAGE

You are not allowed to choose to date, court, or marry your spouse. Anyone who does this and gets married will never be allowed to be gods because god-status can only be achieved when the prophet approves of the marriage through revelation.

Digging deep, she opened the door.

"What are you doing up so early?" Her mother looked up, startled as Becca walked through the door.

"I went outside to think. The snow was beautiful and peaceful," Becca said, trying to calm her frazzled nerves.

"It's freezing outside, and you don't have a jacket on," Mother questioned.

"I don't mind the cold. I like it," Becca said as she lifted her shoulders and walked past her mother like it was no big deal.

To add credibility to the charade, she resisted the urge to shiver as she strolled into the living room in front of Father Arlen, grabbed her blanket, and then marched upstairs to get dressed for church.

As Becca settled into the repetitive Sunday activities, an uneasiness descended. Something just didn't feel right. Rehearsing every moment from the time she walked into her house from the biting cold, she searched for clues as to if her parents knew what she had done. They had said nothing to make her believe they held suspicions.

Mother barely even looked at her throughout the day, but that could have been normal as it was her Sunday to cook the family meal. Father was busy as well with his Sunday duties. Unable to find evidence to support her feeling, Becca reasoned it away with the fact that she was just exhausted from the lack of sleep the night before.

Later that night, she made her way to her balcony, hoping for a page in case Mac wanted to check in before he left. Thankful for the open extension of her room that gave her the illusion of freedom, she turned on her pager, fixed her eyes on the road below and watched for Mac's truck. She planned on waiting there until family evening prayer.

"Becca, would you come to my room?" Mother's voice on the intercom made her jump. That intercom. When they first moved into the house, she had been so excited to use it. Now it only served to make her world smaller.

It was strange to be called into her mother's room right before family prayer. She was usually downstairs at this time corralling the younger children.

Just as Becca stood up, her pager went off. She rushed to her closet, took it off, and hid it under some clothes. Thankful it hadn't buzzed when she was with her mother, Becca made her way down the hall.

Father was standing at the door as she entered, and politely invited her in. Immediately Becca knew something was wrong. Behind her, Father closed the door, placed a chair in front of it, and sat down.

She sat on the edge of the bed. Mother sat solemnly next to her in the side chair. Father looked down at his hands squeezed tightly together, shaking faintly. When he looked up, he said, "We know you have another pager."

Teeth clenched, Becca sat silent.

"You are not a good example to the other children, Becca..."

Guilt flooded in. She dearly loved her other younger siblings and never wanted to harm them by her behaviors. She also knew her, and Mac's choices had put Mac in a position of losing his home and never being able to come back to the Crick. The heaviness of being caught wasn't just about her getting in trouble. If it were just her getting in trouble, then it wouldn't bother her so intensely.

"…and you are hurting your mother horribly," he continued.

Tears flowed at the truth of his statement. Love was too small a word to describe how she felt towards her selfless mother.

All at once, anger replaced sadness. No matter what Becca did, she would lose. Strict obedience would require her to hand over her future. She would end up like Tilly, married and unable to live as she wished. If she followed her heart and will to choose her life course, then she was bad, hurting her siblings and her mother.

"We know you are sneaking out to see that damn boy!" Father said, shaking as her mother cried silently behind her.

They knew.

Her ears started to ring, and she noticed her jaw was clenched and her teeth were locked shut. She felt as if a vice was all around her and she was being squeezed, unable to move.

"You'll not leave this room until you give us that damn pager," Father fumed. It was unlike him to curse, and Becca could tell he was trying to restrain his anger.

Eyes locked in space, Becca sat statue-like on the edge of the bed. All three sat in silence and time stood still.

After what seemed like hours, Father stood and declared, "Fine, if you won't give it up, I will tear your whole room apart while you stay in here with your mother."

That was it, she was broken and had to give in. If he tore her room apart, he would surely find it, and she would not have a chance to read or erase the last message from Mac. Above all, she didn't want to take the chance they would have proof he was the boy she was meeting. He could be kicked out. She had to try to protect him.

"I'll get it," she surrendered and stood in front of Father Arlen.

"Your mother will go with you," he ordered, then moved the chair so she could open the door.

Racing to her room, Becca tried to leave her mother behind so she could somehow erase the message while she grabbed the pager in the closet. The best she could do was take the batteries out as her mother had kept up, and reached for it.

"What are you doin' Becca?" her mother accused, taking it from her hands.

"I'm taking the batteries out so you can't read my messages," she asserted.

It was no use to lie. Truth be told, it didn't matter if she took out the batteries. Once batteries were replaced, they could retrieve the messages anyway. At least the code she and Mac maintained would keep most of the meaning cryptic. She had that to cling to. But the number could be traced back to him without difficulty. His fate was in her parent's hands. If the prophet found out, there wasn't a thing anyone could do to keep him in town.

Rushing passed her mother, she grabbed her blue flashlight and raced to her door.

"Where are you goin'?" Becca ignored her mother's voice and ran downstairs and out of the house.

Reaching for her bike, she hopped on and rode. It was already dark, but navigation was not a problem. If there was a way, she would have ridden her bike all the way to Riverton to her dad's. But that was impossible. Someone would probably be out to find her soon anyway.

The Crick was eerily quiet as it was Sunday and families were inside praying and resting. The whole community was full of people who said they loved her, but she wondered if they loved her, or the thought of who they expected her to be. The weight of years of the Prophet's expectations smothered her from every direction.

She yearned to choose whose hand she held on her wedding day. It wasn't like she wanted to kill or hurt someone. She didn't even want to disobey the prophet's other teachings, but with her feelings for Mac, she couldn't bear to be placed in marriage with someone other than him.

Tears fell as she pedaled further and further out, across the freeway and toward the airport. She had to get away from the community that was supposed to protect her from harm.

The airport road was a long, dark, road with no street lights. Directed by the small blue flashlight, she pedaled hard and fast, struggling to breathe through forceful, angry, tears. Barely able to see in front of her face, she finally stopped, laid her bike down, and sat on the side of the road. Tears that had fallen for hours betrayed her as she tried to cry but couldn't. She tried to scream, but her voice, too, betrayed her, and wouldn't let out a sound.

It would be such a relief if Mac would somehow drive by and whisk her away. It would be done. But she knew that wouldn't happen. Every Sunday he was getting ready to leave town for the work week. He would not be able to get away.

After sitting for what seemed like hours, she realized she had no clue what to do, so she picked herself up and pedaled back toward town. Without the distraction of the dense emotions just moments before, fear crept into her heart and trickled down her back on the dark, lonely road.

As if on cue, cries of coyotes cackled in the near distance, mocking her with their eerie screams in the darkness. It was impossible to see where they were, but their yelps surrounded her in the desert, and she resisted the urge to keep turning her gaze over her shoulder.

There was no stopping. The only thing she could do was get away from them and find her way back into town. Lifting her chin, she ignored the yelps and screams.

I must keep moving. I must keep moving. I must find safety, and then I will figure this out.

Relief flooded in as she approached the edge of town and felt some space between herself and the pack. Although they still sounded in the distance, she was safe enough. Several police cars were parked on the side of the road ahead, so to avoid them, she hid in the darkness and stayed on the other side of tall fences instead of the middle of the street. There was no way she could know if they were looking for her but didn't want to take the chance.

She did not want to talk to anyone. The police were all men from the church. Some were even her own blood uncles who would not have sympathy for her. Any disobedience would affect their personal connection to the will of the prophet.

Completely numb, she propped her bike in its spot on the side of her house and entered the quiet home through the front door. All the lights were off, and she noticed the clock on the wall read past midnight.

Determined to somehow figure out how to make her life work, she climbed the stairs without regard for any creaks or sounds, relieved she didn't have to elude the truth of being out. Too exhausted to change into her pajamas, she laid fully clothed on her bed and fell asleep.

She awoke in the morning determined to get a message to Mac to warn him of the possible outcome, so she dressed and readied to go to work. Without saying a word to anyone, she slipped out the kitchen side door and took off to work on her bike.

After riding for a few minutes, Father Arlen and Jerusha drove by and stopped to ask if she wanted a ride. Ignoring them, she turned her head. Unsure if Jerusha knew what had happened, Becca felt slightly guilty, but Father Arlen could fill her in if he needed to. Once at work, she was able to use the phone to send Mac a quick message to let him know the pager was gone.

Jerusha wore a puzzled face across from her as they worked, but Becca refused to talk about it. If she had learned anything from the last few days, it was that she had to keep moving forward to stay ahead of the circumstances that were screaming at her. Trying to figure out what to do had put her into such darkness, her head hurt.

The urges her parents had given to pray had fallen on deaf ears. She could no longer pray to do the Prophet's will but knew she had to pray for something. Remembering a talk Uncle Rulon had given about asking for knowledge, she decided to do that instead. Knowledge was neutral and didn't depend so much on opinions from old men.

***

"Becca, you got a letter," Mother handed her a white envelope decorated with hearts and flowers.

It had been over a week since the pager had been discovered. Each day had mirrored the last as Becca walked zombie-like through her duties. Barely even noticing her other family members, she did what she had to do and spent the rest of her time in her room. Wishing she could climb out of her own skin, Becca settled into a dark place without knowing where comfort would come.

"Oh, it's from Stacy!" Becca took the treasure.

Mother beamed, "I miss Stacy. I just love that girl."

Stacy had been one of the brightest parts of her early days at the Crick. Somewhere along the way, they had lost touch with each other. She had gotten married and moved to Canada right after Becca started working with Levi at the Crick. Becca rarely heard from her, so any correspondence was magical.

Only two pages, the letter seemed short, and Becca hung on every word. Stacy had twin babies and a two-year-old with a disability. Her sister-in-law and brother had moved in with them and were helping her a great deal. She ended with, "I love you," and, "you should come see us sometime."

It was like a hug. For a moment, Becca recognized a feeling. It was something she hadn't felt in a long time.

It was hope. She had an idea.

"Mother, I think I know what I should do. I need to get away. I really think if I can get away, then when I come back, I may be over this."

"Oh Becca, but where would you go?" Mother seemed genuinely interested in anything Becca could do that would make her better.

"Canada! Stacy would let me come stay for a while. I could go to church at the Blackmore Compound, and I could help Stacy with her babies and house. I will work extra hours for a couple of weeks to help save money for the trip, then maybe you and Father could take me?"

Mother stared into the distance, "I trust Stacy, and I think it would be really good for you to get away for a little bit. We could, maybe, see if there's someone headed to Canada. You could ride with them and stay for a few weeks, then see how you're doin'…"

"I just need to get away, so I don't have temptation, Mother. I know it'd be so good for me. I think I'd come back a better girl," Becca reassured.

"I'll talk it over with Father Arlen," Mother agreed.

Just a few weeks later, Becca bundled up in her warmest clothes, loaded her suitcase in the van, and settled into her seat. It was January, and cold, but January cold in Arizona was very different than January cold in Canada.

Different was what she needed. Hopeful the change would turn the nightmare her life had become around one way or another, Becca felt better than she had in a long time. Her only regret was that she had no way to communicate to Mac what was going on or where she would be.

Desiree knew everything, though, and promised to somehow get him the message. Becca was incredibly grateful for the fact that her parents had not turned Mac in. They knew he would be kicked out and had compassion for him.

Mother and Father had decided to take her themselves and see to her safety. It was a 16-hour drive. Becca had been so excited preparing the night before that she had hardly slept, so she took advantage of the night-drive to sleep most of the way. Father Arlen and Mother took turns driving, and they only stopped for bathroom breaks and food.

When she awoke in the morning, they were still driving. Raising her messy head, she looked out the window to find green fields covered in light snow. Beyond the fields was a blanket of tall, dark green trees. Just after the trees was a dark blue mountain with snow-capped heights.

"Welcome to Canada, Becca," Mother beamed. It was nice to see her smile.

Awed by the flawless white snow separated by spots of vivid green trees and purple and blue mountains, Becca praised, "It's beautiful."

"We should be to Bountiful within a few hours," Father announced.

"Fix yourself up, the Bishop will be there to welcome us," Mother reminded.

A long uphill, open driveway lead to the bishop's home. Bundled children playing in the snow waved at the van, and several mothers carrying babies or pushing small ones in strollers stood watch as the older children played. It was a happy, whimsical sight.

For a moment Becca wished she could go back to the days of just playing outside with cousins and siblings. But that was impossible. Not even the prophet himself could turn back time. She smiled as a young girl caught her eye and waved.

Several older girls ran up to the van and offered to help them unload. Just a few moments later, Bishop Blackmore drove up and invited them to come inside. The entryway took them to a large room with rows and rows of tables.

Father explained to the Bishop that they were there to bring Becca to visit with Stacy's family. He asked if they could stay a night before heading back to the Crick. Becca watched the bishop's face to see if he was as kind as she had heard him to be. He listened intently to her Father and kindly invited them to eat and stay the night without a second thought.

One of the many mothers showed them the bathroom so they could freshen up for dinner. For the time being, they left their belongings next to a window in the entryway. After washing, Becca watched as small children and young teens filled the rows and rows of benches around the tables.

Teen daughters and mothers brought out plates to serve the younger children and everyone enjoyed a happy meal with the Bishop sitting at the head of the table. Becca lost count of the mothers and didn't even try to figure it out. It was hard to imagine having that many siblings. How did they keep so happy and orderly? The whole scene seemed like pure magic.

Once dinner was finished, Becca, Mother, and Father followed the bishop around his home and property as he pointed out his orchards and garden areas. Several orchards with rows and rows of leafless fruit trees covered the land, and every so often Becca saw tires swings and gazebos that were slowly attracting children who were finished washing after the dinner meal.

Becca imagined how beautiful the area would be in the summer months. With that many trees, there would be incredible amounts of fruit and the expansive garden areas would, no doubt, yield hundreds of pounds of vegetables.

Several yards past the enormous home was a little cottage where guests could stay. When the bishop left them to the small retreat, Father and Mother melted into the bed, exhausted from the drive.

Becca wasn't nearly as tired as they were, so she went to sit on the front steps of the cottage to think. The cold wind hit her cheeks, so she bundled her arms together and pulled her hood over her head to keep warm. The air in Canada was crisper than the Crick air for sure.

Guilt crept in as she realized her parents had a long day ahead as they were heading back. Despite all the grief Becca had given them, they loved her deeply and wanted the best for her. She knew that and hoped this trip would provide the change her life needed.

Three options swirled in her mind. She was determined to choose one once and for all, then do it without looking back. The first option was to lose any desires she had for Mac along with the right to choose her future, and then find a way to be at peace with the Prophet's will.

The second option was to find a way to make Mac a part of her future without disobeying the prophet.

The third option, one she barely allowed to surface, was to somehow leave the Crick and escape it all. But that meant she would never be welcomed in her own home the same. She would become an apostate.

16

CRACKING THE CODE
2002

CODE OF CONDUCT: KEEPING SWEET

Your very life depends on if you've kept sweet. No matter what happens, always keep sweet.

"Stacy!" Becca rushed out to greet her friend.

"Becca Sue, Louie Blue!"

"Awe, you remembered my nickname!"

"How could I forget? You practically ran the Golden Circle."

"You know it!" Becca boasted.

Mother joined in the conversation with questions about family and how it was to live in Canada until Father Arlen reminded them of the time.

"We need to get going, we have a long drive ahead of us."

"You take good care of my girl now Stacy," Mother smiled.

"I think it'll be the other way around," Stacy teased, and Mother and Father climbed into the van and pulled away.

Cautious as to how much to share with Stacy about Mac, Becca spoke about work and church as they drove to her house. Just to test the water, Becca threw out the fact that she had been in a little trouble for being interested in a boy and carefully watched Stacy's reaction to see if she was against it. Her face remained the same, but Becca decided to change the subject anyway.

"I'm sorry, am I talking too much? I haven't even asked about you!"

"No, it's ok. I'm just thankful we have a minute to talk before I get back to the children. Courtney is watching them while the guys work. You will like Courtney." Courtney was Stacy's sister-in-law who had moved in.

"Oh, I can't wait to see them," Becca said.

Stacy smiled, lifted her shoulders, and said, "Well, I do make some cute babies! They grow up quick, though. Before I know it, they'll be wearing aprons six times too big and climbing up onto my cupboards putting dishes away."

Becca laughed at the thought. She had almost forgotten about that.

"Hey, you remember how I used to come and stay the night at your house, and we would listen to country music?" Becca reminisced.

"We were so bad."

"I thought it was so fun," Becca responded, trying to determine where Stacy stood.

"You know what I think is fun? I think while you are here, we should color our hair with henna," Stacy offered.

Becca nodded, "Yes, and make some good desserts and eat way too much."

"Done," she said, lifting her chin with satisfaction.

"Thank you for letting me come," Becca said.

"Of course! We will have so much fun and not think about a thing back home," Stacy promised.

The last comment made her wonder how much Mother had shared. Certainly, her mother would have told Stacy about the struggles she was going through before allowing her to stay. Becca longed to open up and ask but wanted to start off on the right foot. She was feeling better and didn't want to ruin it with the possibility of any disapproval.

***

Becca acclimated quickly to Stacy's house and her children. The business of meals and bath times was not foreign to her, and she helped just the same as if it were her own family. Sitting idle was not her way, and every day they made food and enjoyed moments of creativity.

Courtney, Stacy's sister-in-law, was an instant friend who seemed like a comfortable shoe. She was just a couple of years older than Becca and had lived at the Crick before moving to Canada. Every once in a while, she and Becca had moments alone to talk, and Becca felt like she could share her secret.

"Courtney, I'm here because I've been sneaking out with a boy, and I'm scared Uncle Warren will place me in marriage and kick him out," Becca opened up because she just couldn't hold it in any longer.

Courtney listened with a knowing look on her face. "Becca, has Stacy not told you any of my stories?"

"No, just that you and Marshall moved in here and that Marshall works with Stephan."

"Well, we started out kind of like you guys. We fell in love, and our parents did not approve either. But, we had heard that Bishop Blackmore was marrying couples who had gone through a repentance process."

Courtney explained how they had fallen in love at the Crick and struggled with wanting to be together. She, too, had lived with the fear of Marshall being sent away, and the ever-present possibility she might be placed in marriage to someone else. Everything Becca was walking through, Courtney had walked through a few years before.

"We weren't allowed to talk about any of it to anyone but our parents," Courtney looked out the window. "I'm sure Stacy knows some of it, but she doesn't know it all."

"Well, I didn't exactly tell her everything about me coming. I don't know how much my Mother told her either," Becca explained.

Becca drank in every detail Courtney shared. Step by step, Courtney traced the path she and Marshall followed so Becca could possibly do the same and marry Mac without forsaking the prophet and the religion.

"Marshall and I had to repent, get re-baptized, keep our distance from one another and pray for an answer. We also had to prove to our parents that we were pure and ready to be placed in marriage. And we had to keep quiet about all of it. Not very many people knew what was going on. Just our parents and the Bishop."

It sounded so complicated and lengthy. Becca was both encouraged and discouraged at the same time.

"Marshall had to regain his priesthood along the way too. Then, and only then, with both sets of our parents in agreement, we were able to meet with the Bishop again to see if he would marry us. We had heard that some other young people had approached him, and he married them, so we did too."

"And he married you!" Becca almost yelled in excitement.

"But Becca, if you are going to try to do it, you need to be very careful to go about it the right way. You'll need to set up an appointment with the Bishop soon, and you'll need to get your parent's approval."

"As soon as I hear from Mother, I'll try to set it up and make it look like we just wanted to say goodbye to the bishop in private," Becca planned.

If her mother knew there was a possibility she could do this and still be accepted by the prophet and the community, maybe she would be ok with it.

Surely she would want me to be happy.

"I can help you set up the meeting," Courtney offered.

"Really! Oh, Courtney thank you so much!" Becca hugged Courtney just as Stacy walked in.

"Why are you two so huggy?" She teased.

"I just love this girl," Courtney joined in.

"Didn't you know we were long-lost BFF's?" Becca said, reaching for Stacy to squeeze her too. She wanted to tell Stacy everything but didn't know if she should just yet. It would be a cruel joke if Stacy discouraged the new-found hope she held.

Becca knew what to do. Ironically, the trip to Canada, which was supposed to put more distance in between her and Mac had actually brought her closer to the possibility of being with him. If Courtney and Marshall could do it, then they could too.

***

With the knowledge of a possibility of being able to marry Mac, Becca relaxed and allowed herself to just have fun. Playing with Stacy's children, Hockey games, henna hair, and gooey treats took up her days and nights, and she felt the hope that living without fear can bring.

Each Sunday they went to church, and Becca noticed the people seemed less stiff-nosed than those at the Crick. She also saw friends from grade school who had gotten married in Canada. More and more she felt at home in a place that seemed to be an answer to her every problem.

Before she knew it, the time had come for her to go back to the Crick. Courtney, true to her word, helped her to set up a meeting with the Bishop. Becca had decided not to tell her parents about the meeting until they were all at the compound together in case they refused to hear the details. She hoped the kind Bishop would see her side and convince her parents there was a possibility that she and Mac could be together.

Just a few days later, Becca and her parents sat in the bishop's office with looks of total confusion as he asked them what the meeting was for.

Before her parents could speak, Becca boldly interjected, "I found out that there have been some people my age who have come to Canada to be married."

Shock replaced confusion and her Mother looked at Father and then back at the bishop.

"...and, I was wondering if we could maybe talk about how it could be done, and you could tell my parents how it could be done. I could, maybe, with Father and Mother's permission stay here and repent some more..."

Still shocked by the whole exchange, her parents sat speechless until Becca mentioned staying longer.

"Becca, you can't stay longer. We spent all our extra money just getting' you here and comin' back to bring you home. We will not leave here without you..." Father sputtered.

"Let me stop you there," the Bishop broke into the awkward exchange.

"The last time I married someone from the Crick, I decided it would be the last. The only way you can be married, Becca is if the Prophet himself gave me permission. It is no longer available for me to make those kinds of decisions."

"But we would do anything you told us to do. We would repent and stay away from each other..."

"I am so sorry, but I just can't do anything the prophet doesn't endorse. I would if I could. But I just can't," he comforted.

Numb, Becca looked at him and willed back tears. She could see he was conflicted and cared deeply.

Father stood and apologized, "We are sorry to take up your time, Bishop."

"Thank you so much for your time," Mother responded with a forced smile, standing with Father.

Unable to move, Becca sat until Father Arlen spoke up, "Come on, Becca, we're goin' home."

She stared at the Bishop's face and could see something she didn't understand. His eyes were kind, and his mouth was drawn in a straight line. He looked away from Becca's stare as her parents ushered her out the door.

You look like you want to help me. Why can't you just help me?

Becca thought the words but didn't dare ask. Instead, she picked up her suitcase, closed her eyes briefly, lifted her chin, and stepped out of the office in defeat without looking back.

For the first few hours, the ride home was silent. No one wanted to talk. Father Arlen drove as Mother took a short nap. They had traveled for hours without a night's rest, and after the exchange with the Bishop, it was easy to see they were exhausted.

"I can help you drive, Father," Becca spoke up, trying to mend the tension.

"I might have to take you up on that," he answered dully and pulled over, so she could drive for a bit.

She wasn't entirely new to driving but was still nervous behind the wheel. Father had to be completely worn out to trust her abilities, mainly since she had only driven at the Crick. Once she was well on her way, he laid down to take a nap, and her Mother woke up.

"Well, it's Becca driving," she said and yawned.

"Yep, and I haven't run into anything yet either," Becca teased, trying to keep things light.

"Let me know when you need me to take over, I got a little rest and can do some driving too," she encouraged.

"Mother, I'm sorry to have surprised you with the meeting with the Bishop. I just learned about Courtney and Marshall and thought if the Bishop could help us you'd want to know," Becca tried to explain.

Mother looked out the window, paused and said, "I just feel like I am losing you, Becca."

Her words hit hard. Choked with emotion, Becca wanted to tell her she was wrong, that she would always be her girl. How could her desire to choose her future ever change the fact that they were Mother and daughter? There was so much she wanted to say, but it would only make her mother worry more.

"You can't lose me, I'm right here," Becca forced a smile and watched the road.

"There's more than one way to lose a person," Mother continued.

Becca was aware of what she meant. It was her worst nightmare. In a perfect world, she could have her mother and the ability to choose her life. They would all live happy lives and still be a part of the church. But that wasn't the way the prophet or the church operated, and they both knew it.

***

"Go without me, I'm still not done with my hair. I'll just walk to church when I'm ready," Becca explained as she looked at her reflection in the mirror. Mother hesitated, not wanting to get into a fight, but openly disturbed by Becca's decision.

"Becca, just put it in a braid and hustle," Mother encouraged.

"I will just give me a bit. And as soon as it's done, I'll just ride my bike to church."

"Fine, but don't take long and come sit with the family. We'll save you a seat," Mother replied.

Aside from braiding Becca's hair herself, her Mother had no choice but to go.

Grateful for a moment alone, Becca took to braiding and puffing, braiding and puffing. Looking at her reflection, she remembered how Tilly used to tell her what a brat she was because she fixed her hair in front of the mirror.

At the time, Becca had felt bad about herself like she was conceited. Finishing the braid, she was happy for the chance to just relax and enjoy getting ready. Her hair was the one thing she had control over, and it would do anything she told it to do.

Her strained efforts to look nice was on the off chance Mac would be in church. It was her first Sunday back, and she was anxious to share what she had learned in Canada. Despite the Bishop's denial of her wishes to marry them and her parent's complete disapproval, she still held hope that there was something they could do. If Marshall and Courtney could do it through prayer and repentance, surely she and Mac could convince Uncle Warren and do the same.

Once her hair was done, she reached for her hidden notebook and pulled out 3 carefully penned pages written the night before. Folding the note carefully, she put it in her bag, walked out of the house, and made her way to the church. Whether Mac would be a part of her day or not, she had to get him the message about Canada. Her only hope was to be brave and talk to Uncle Warren and somehow convince him.

Just as she had thought, the building was full, and church had already begun. Despite her urge to find a seat in the back, she strained to find her family. Her Mother looked relieved to see her when she sat down by Jerusha and pulled out a notebook.

Scanning the crowd searching for Mac, she took notice of who was sitting by who since all new brides would be sitting next to their husbands. After being gone for weeks in Canada, surely there would be some new brides.

Her heart pounded in her chest as she recognized a sandy-brown head. Mac was sitting with his family. It was nice to see him, even if it was the back of his head. But she was a little disappointed. Without eye contact, she had no way of communicating. She continued the scan of the church, and her breath caught in her throat as she noticed Mac's sister was sitting next to her stepdad.

Surely that isn't right. She can't be married to her own stepfather.

There had to be another reason she was sitting next to him. Her mind raced.

Why would the prophet place someone just a few years older than me in marriage to a stepfather who was twice her age? Why would the prophet do that?

As church service ended, Becca watched as the whole family stood and, sure enough, it was Mac's step-sister. It was his stepfather. They were married. Mac's step-sister was now his own stepmother. Never in a thousand years would she have believed that was even possible. Her mind churned.

If the prophet would do that, then what would keep him from placing me in marriage to Father Arlen?

Happy, righteous families walked past Becca, and she felt as if she was going to throw up. It was wrong for her to question the prophet, and no one else seemed to be slightly disturbed. It reminded her of the day Tilly was married but worse. Becca's eyes were now open to the possibility of what lay ahead. She couldn't do it. She couldn't. As much as she loved her mother, loved the Crick and her family, and even loved her church, she couldn't trust her future to the Prophet's will.

Concerned, Jerusha touched Becca's shoulder, "Come on, Becca, it's time to go. You ok?"

Dazed, she looked at Jerusha and lied, "Oh, I'm ok."

Nothing was ok. Nothing.

Just as Mac walked past, she caught his eye, and he scratched his nose. She knew he would be looking for her later.

***

After finding out that Mac's sister was married to his stepfather, Becca could think of nothing else. Rushing through the Sunday dinner dishes, she was determined to go find Mac.

Several brothers and sisters played innocently on the carport, skating and riding bikes, and as she walked past them, no one even noticed. The sun had not set as she hopped onto her bike and frantically pedaled into town looking for him. It would be a good couple of hours before family prayer, so she felt confident there was enough time to at least find him, and give him the note. Meeting during the day was a huge risk, but she didn't have the luxury of time to wait until evening because he had to head out of town to work.

She made her way through town past the candy shop and over the creek bridge way. Rounding the corner toward Cottonwood park, she spotted his truck. Cruising toward the church at a snail-like pace, he was just beyond the windy, red-sandy reservoir roads. He was looking for her too. Heading the same direction, but careful to stay far enough away, Becca pedaled toward the old reservoir.

Out of breath from pedaling, Becca lowered her bike. The sand had made it hard to move, so she decided to just hike instead. Mac parked on the other side of the hill. She followed the path down the windy, sandy trail into an opening on the other side into a wash area.

If it wasn't daytime, Becca might have yelled his name but didn't want to draw any attention, so she just followed the trail. He turned to her as she reached the sand opening down by the wash, surrounded by trees.

When they were close enough to hear each other with low voices, Becca handed him the note and said, "I have so much to tell you, but I don't have much time."

"I have to hurry too, I think someone is following us," he said taking her hand and the note it held.

"Did your sister marry your father?" Becca had to ask, even though she already knew the answer.

Mac let go of her hand and replied, "Yeah, she did."

"I just don't understand. That'd be like me marrying Father Arlen. I can't believe that could happen. That the prophet would do that," Becca said feeling unusually vulnerable talking to him face to face during the light of day.

Suddenly his eyes looked beyond her, his face turned from concern to stone. Twirling around, she saw Father Arlen making his way up the sandy path. His face was red, and he was panting.

"Mac, would a priesthood man be meeting up with girls?" Father Arlen yelled as he rushed forward with shaking hands and drawn eyebrows.

"No," Mac said without fear or concern. He stepped toward Father Arlen with his hands in his pockets and stared him straight in the eye.

He would give it all up for our relationship. For us.

Admiration for this man who had become one of her best friends welled inside of Becca. She felt a trust that wasn't entirely present before and knew he would be brave and stand next to her no matter what.

"This time, I'll be reporting this to Uncle Warren and your father…"

"Ok. Do that!" Mac countered leaning in towards him one last time. He looked at Becca, then turned around and walked away.

Right then, Becca was his. It was as if the exchange itself connected them beyond words or actions. He gave it all up. She would too. Every part of her wanted to follow Mac down that hill and leave Father Arlen, but she knew it wasn't time.

Her blood boiled as she turned and walked opposite of everything she wanted.

"I am very disappointed with you, Becca. After all we've done to get you through this. I've lost all my trust in you," he declared.

There wasn't a thing he could say at that point that would make her change her mind, and Becca tried not to let the words soak in too much.

They made their way down the path, and he lifted her bike and put it in the back of his truck. Father had definitely had enough. Becca could tell by his shaking hands which he didn't even try to control, this time was different. She knew better than to try to smooth anything over and didn't have the energy to do it anyway. Mother was going to be devastated. If nothing else, though, Becca had tried to be sweet by going to Canada. It was all out now. Father knew it was Mac. A meeting with Uncle Warren was inevitable.

"Becca, I'm taking away your bike until further notice," Father said as the truck came to a stop outside of their home.

That was her bike. It was her freedom. Her dad had given it to her, and no one could touch it. Words swirled around in her head, but not one made its way to her mouth.

The all too familiar feeling of being trapped, unable to move enveloped her. He turned the truck off, opened his door and took the bike without a word. In that, he was right. This was no time for words.

***

Becca felt a gentle tug on her arm, and she turned over in her bed to see her mother. "Father set up an appointment with Uncle Warren, so you'll stay home from work today."

Becca closed her eyes, took a breath and said, "Fine," then laid still staring at the ceiling.

"We love you so much Becca, the prophet knows what's best. If only you could see that. He has your best interests at heart and meeting up with that boy isn't in your best interest."

"You have to believe how precious you are to your Heavenly Father, he's the only one who can forgive you, but you have to choose to change your path."

She could tell her mother genuinely believed those words. If only she could.

Before she thought it out, Becca opened her mouth and sleepily said, "What's in my best interest, Mother? Is marrying a man I don't even know in my best interest? How'd it be if the prophet married me to Father Arlen like he married Mary Cook to her stepfather?"

"I don't think that would happen to you. You have to trust the prophet, and everything will work out," her Mother tried to reassure.

Becca rolled out of bed and walked into the bathroom. They might as well be speaking different languages.

"I have to shower. I'll be down in a little bit," Becca said.

"Ok. Don't make us late. It's gonna be alright, Becca you'll see," Mother continued.

You'll see. You'll see.

They both looked at the exact same circumstances and saw entirely different realities. How could anything ever be alright? Her Mother was supposed to protect her from harm, and it seemed she was pushing her right into it without even knowing.

17

AFTER MEETING WITH WARREN: LETTING GO OF THE CODE
MARCH 2002   AGE 18

CODE OF CONDUCT: BOYS AND GIRLS

Upon the prophet's instruction, I have been told that any young man or boy choosing to flirt is to be sent away from us before they soil our girls. Ladies, don't be pulled in by their tricks. It would be a sad day if you were caught being wooed by sneaky boys trying to get you to pay attention to them.

My name is in the black book. My name. The black book.

Shaken by the exchange with Uncle Warren and shivering from the icy, long walk to the Spud Pit, Becca lifted her vibrating hand to the phone on the wall and dialed Mac's number.

Uncle Warren knew. Soon the prophet would know too. Mac was kicked out. A little black book had her name in it. There was nothing anyone could do to stop the momentum that had gathered. Nothing.

Whatever motive Uncle Warren had for allowing her to leave through the back door, she couldn't imagine, but was thankful for the moment to slip away to gather her thoughts. She had to talk to Mac and make a plan. Remembering Uncle Warren's words, "You are old enough to be placed in marriage," she cringed and waited for Mac to answer the phone.

"Mac, I just got done talking to Uncle Warren. He said you lost the priesthood," Becca pushed the words out before he could even say hello.

"I'm not allowed back into town unless I check in first," Mac was as calm as if she was making small talk. It was part of her attraction to him in the first place, but at this point, she had no patience for calm.

"…I think I might just go camp in the woods for a while and figure out what to do next…"

Interrupting, Becca raised her voice, "Mac, you can't leave me. By the time you're able to come back, I'd be married to someone else!"

"Well, I have to live somewhere. I'm just sayin' I'll camp until I figure it out…"

"I don't want you to leave. I'd never see you again," Becca reasoned.

After a long pause in which neither one knew what to say, Mac offered an idea.

"Do you think your dad might help us?"

The phone went silent as Becca considered the idea. Her dad, of all people, had to know what it felt like to lose the priesthood. And, more than that, he loved her. He was smart and cared about her future. He had seemed protective over Tilly when she was married without his knowledge.

"I want to say yes. I think he'll understand. Maybe we could stay with him for a while until we figure it all out," Becca knew once she decided to involve Travis there would be no backing down. There was no other way.

"Give me 2 weeks to figure out work," Mac said.

"Two weeks is too long. Anything could happen in two weeks," Becca panicked.

"Becca, I have to figure out work. I'll need my last paycheck," he continued.

"But we need a plan before that," Becca interrupted.

To calm her mind, he offered, "Maybe you can take some of your things and hide them by the side of the building at the Spud Pit. I'll come and pick them up at night and keep them in the back of my truck until we can leave for good. If you talk to your dad and he's ok with it, then I'll pick you up, and we'll head to his house."

For the first time since she was nine, Becca was thankful her dad lived in Riverton and not at the Crick. She had never even considered the possibility of living in the old house again and calling it home. Grateful her dad had insisted on keeping a relationship with them, she felt endeared to him all the more now knowing that his insistence on remaining connected was what may allow her to leave.

"I'll call him now. I don't know when I'll be able to call you again, but I'll give my dad your number, and, and... don't even think about leavin' for good without me!"

"I won't," he assured.

Becca hung up. A new excitement started to form. It was possible she just might be able to be with Mac. She had a new momentum and needed to keep it, so she dialed her dad.

Through the receiver, she could hear the 4th, 5th, and then 6th ring.

"Pick up, dad, pick up," she urged into the phone just as his answering machine turned on and encouraged a message after the beep.

"Hi dad, it's Becca. I guess you're busy. I'll call you back when I can." Docking the phone, she leaned her forehead against the wall.

At least there was a little time to think about how to approach him. If this was going to work at all, she had to be sure he would not tell anyone.

***

Thankful for so many brothers and sisters in the house, Becca sat around the dinner table that evening almost anonymous as Father Arlen offered prayer. Opening her eyes brazenly, she peered at the obedient, closed-eyed faces surrounding the table.

How can I be sitting here knowing what I am going to do and yet they know nothing?

A familiar sensation of unsettled emotions caused her belly to churn.

Father Arlen and her Mothers were the only ones who knew about her meeting with Uncle Warren. After leaving the meeting through the back door, there was no way for her to know what Uncle Warren had told them.

Did they know Mac was kicked out? Did Uncle Warren talk to them about placing me in marriage?

No one even said a word when she walked through the kitchen door after secretly speaking to Mac at the Spud Pit. She had gone straight to her room without even a sideways look from Mother Susan.

Father Arlen finished the prayer, and all eyes opened. Jerusha smiled sweetly to her left as she passed a plate of bread and the younger children chattered. Except for the forced smile on her mother's face, it was as if nothing had happened at all.

The rhythm of their family rituals took over, and before she knew it, Becca was in her room getting ready for bed when the phone rang downstairs, and Mother Susan called to Becca over the intercom.

"Becca, Travis is on the phone."

Jerusha looked up from her scripture reading. It wasn't usual for him to call, especially that late. He only called when they had a planned trip or a weekend visit coming up. Wishing she hadn't left him a message, Becca rushed downstairs. There would be no way for her to communicate what she wanted from home. Especially with Mother Susan standing right beside her.

As if the very act of speaking to Travis was a chore, Mother Susan stood in the kitchen holding the phone awkwardly with one hand while perching her other hand on her hip. A few curious little brothers and sisters gathered behind her with accusing eyes. A call from Travis was a controversial thing, and they loved to be in on the action. Rolling her eyes, Becca took the phone and spoke while the audience kept watch.

"Hi, Travis. Oh, yeah. I just wanted to ask you when you were coming to the Crick, and I didn't want to make plans if you were coming," Becca lied.

It was all she could think of that would not arouse suspicion. Cautious to not be on the phone too long, she nervously took control of the conversation.

"Ok well, I need to go. I was headed to bed. Bye."

Whether Travis felt like something was up or not, she couldn't tell. It didn't matter. She just needed to get off and find a way to speak with him later. Hanging the phone on its hook, she turned her attention to Mother Susan.

"Good night, Mother Susan."

"It will be if the phone stops ringing this late and wakin' my children," she said, turning to her children, herding them off to bed.

Jerusha was asleep by the time Becca returned. There was so much to think about. Travis was the only missing part of her plan. Surely he would help her and keep the secret until it was time to go. She would just have to call him from work during her break.

Sleep came in waves, and when she did drift off, dreams about a phone call with news from the prophet and a wedding dress tortured her. In the darkness, she laid on her bed comforting herself with the dad-plan and wished morning would come so she could do something about it.

Jerusha was already dressed and helping the younger children get ready when Becca woke up. She was late. Despite her eagerness to get up early, the sleepless night had taken over, and she had gotten about two hours of sleep just before the sun came up.

An envelope with dainty, pink roses was lying on her bedside table. Recognizing Jerusha's handwriting, Becca smiled. Jerusha had been quiet since dinner and, kind to her core, didn't pry into what was going on.

Anxious to read the note, Becca took it to the bathroom and closed the door.

Dear Becca,

I've been thinking about you a lot lately. I feel like you are having a hard time. It's hard to see you sad. I feel like when you go with Travis then when you come home everyone treats you like you are a bad person. Well, I don't think like everyone else. I just feel sorry for you, because you probably love him very much. I can tell you feel sorry for him and that you are close to him. That's not bad at all, it's not stupid. I bet it's so hard to see someone you love to go the wrong way. I'm sorry. I'm not ever mad at you, I love you, and I want to be your friend. I don't want you to think you are wicked for going with him.

I love it when we get to hang out together. I don't have a lot of friends so when we can do things together, it's always so fun. I like hearing about your adventures with your friends and hope you think of me as a friend as well as a sister…

Sweet, innocent Jerusha had no clue the depth of what was going on. She thought the primary struggle Becca had was wrapped around Travis. For a moment, Becca felt almost protective of her sweet sister who would no doubt follow whatever the prophet said. Becca longed to tell her everything, but that would only make things worse. Even if she opened up fully, Jerusha would never understand.

Unable to burden her with the truth, Becca left the bathroom and slipped the note into a black bag under her bed that held her precious notebooks, photos, and memories. In just a few days, it would be packed away in Mac's truck waiting for her to start a new life.

***

"Hi, Dad, it's Becca. I'm sorry I had to get off so soon last night. I need to ask you something, but you have to promise you'll keep it a secret from Mother and Father."

It was an abrupt way to begin, but there was no other way. Becca held the phone close and spoke calmly as she watched the day attendant at her desk keep busy. The public line at her job was her first chance to reach out. Even though it was right in front of twenty people who could, at any moment walk past and overhear the conversation, she boldly took the chance.

"Becca, are you ok? You sounded a little worried on the voice message, and last night you seemed in trouble? What's going on?"

"First, dad, I have to know you won't tell anyone. Especially Mother." Before he could even answer, she continued. "I want to leave the Crick. I don't want to get married like they married Tilly."

"Becca, you're always welcome here, but slow down. What's going on?" He reasoned.

"I have a boyfriend named Mac Cook. We've gotten caught a few times together, and we both had to talk to Uncle Warren. He kicked Mac out of town. I want to leave too, dad. I want to leave before they marry me to someone else…I figured you might be able to help us until we can figure out what we need to do. But dad, you can't say anything. Even if you don't help us, please don't say anything."

"I'll keep this between you and me," he assured. "Does Mac have a vehicle?"

Comforted by her Dad's understanding, she calmed down a little.

"Yes, he needs two weeks to finish his construction job in Phoenix…"

"Becca, are you sure this is what you really want? If you leave…" He interrupted.

"Yes. Dad. I can't tell you everything right now. But I know I can't get married to someone I don't know. Please, please don't tell anyone. If anyone knew, they'd try to change my mind, and I don't know if I'd ever be able to get out again."

"I know, Becca, I know. I won't tell anyone. You just be sure this is what you really want. Your mother…" She had to stop him right there. Her mother was the hardest part of it all.

"Dad, I can't talk about that right now, I don't want to get in trouble being on the phone here at work."

"Ok, I'll talk to Mac and get back with you," he promised.

"Thank you, dad, I love you."

"I love you too."

Hanging up, Becca looked at her co-workers standing around the tables. For all they knew, she had been talking about a shopping list with her Mother. Walking over to the table, she picked up the jig and began to load it.

Desiree pulled her headphones off and said, "Who were you talkin' to for so long? Your boyfriend?"

The other girls gasped at the idea, then looked down trying to appear like they weren't listening.

Becca laughed and said, "No, mother just needed some things from the store and wanted me to remind Father."

Desiree looked at her sideways. She knew it wasn't the truth but also knew better than to pry under the noses of several other girls. Becca couldn't take the chance of telling Desiree what was going on. If even the slightest hint of this got out, she would never be able to pull it off.

A surge of energy surfaced after she spoke with her dad. It was as if it was already done. There was no other way but to leave. Nothing would change her mind. Nothing could. She loaded another lanyard on a jig and started to plan. All she had to do was create a few last memories with her friends.

Staying busy would be the only way to soothe her frantic mind until Mac came to pick her up. Refusing to even think about a phone call from the Prophet, she decided to just focus on day to day activities and work while keeping space between her and her Mother.

As if she was reading Becca's mind, Desiree took off her headphones and leaned in, so they could talk a little more privately.

"Hey, me and Rachelle have an idea. We want to do a trip to St. George and take a group picture of us girls."

"Yes, we need to do that!" Becca agreed.

"We could sneak in some pictures of us in our new frog pajamas," she leaned in further, lowering her voice, "and maybe even just our jeans. Rachelle's father might let her drive us."

"Let's try to do it on Rachelle's birthday, next Friday," Becca added. It would be Becca's last day at the Crick, and she couldn't think of a better way to spend it.

"Sounds good to me, if your parents will let you do it that soon," Desiree reminded.

"I think they will." She assured.

Since Mac had been kicked out, Becca had noticed her parents seemed less concerned with her every move. In fact, they seemed eager for her to have fun with her friends.

"Oh, and we can go out to eat…"

Becca listened to Desiree's game plan as if she was watching a movie unfold in front of her. But, instead of being a part of the movie, she was a passive onlooker. For several weeks Rachelle and Desiree had been devising little adventures left and right with or without her.

She had to fight to keep from feeling left out. After all, in a matter of days, she would be left out altogether. It was both gutwrenching and gratifying to know that her last day would be filled with two of her best friends on an adventure wearing pants and no dress.

***

Each night Becca made her way up to her room, filled a black garbage bag with whatever she could take without arousing suspicion, and then stuffed it under her bed. Once a bag was ready, she delivered it to the

Spud Pit while everyone was asleep. Bags had to be light enough for her to transport alone, yet full enough to be worth the delivery.

Before the week was over, she was able to deliver 3 packages full of her treasures. Refusing to think about what could happen if someone other than Mac were to find the bags, she focused on remembering it would only be days before she would see them again. They were more than just things. They represented her life.

One last bag would be put together the night she was leaving for good. It would hold her special blankets and items she needed daily like her brushes and toothbrush. One item, a leopard print blanket she had bought from the Jeff's family would be packed the last night. It was a gift for Mac. Once they both lived off the Crick, he would be able to use it without worry of being caught.

Knowing her time was limited, Becca became especially aware of her smaller brothers and sisters. Friday night after work, she sat on the couch in the living room as Arlinda and Arnella pretended to be horses. Two pink and white checkered dresses romped around making their best horsey sounds. They crawled up over her feet and onto the couch, then jumped to the floor and wrestled. Anyone could see they were best friends. She watched them, enjoying what would have irritated her just days before.

When did they get so big?

Becca wasn't the only one who had been growing. Lost in her own struggles the last two years, she hadn't been in tune with her youngest sisters. A deep pain rose in her gut as she realized those sweet girls were going to grow up and may not even remember her. Worse, the grownups may tell them stories about how she was a bad person. Shame filled her as she remembered believing all the stories about cousins who had left.

Before getting too caught up in the heaviness of that thought, she gave herself a pep talk.

Well, I can't control what they are told, but I can control if I remember them or not. Tomorrow I will take a minute with each of my brothers and sisters and take pictures of them. That way I can never forget how things really were.

Inspired by her great idea, Becca reached out, picked up Arlinda and gave her a big hug.

"When did you get so big?"

"I don't know. I just did," Arlinda looked into Becca's face with her big eyes, gave her a squeeze and then pushed to get away to go play.

Mother joined Becca on the couch just as Arlinda galloped off.

"They are just too cute," Becca said with a faint smile.

"You know who else is cute, Danica," Mother added. "In fact, Tilly is coming over tomorrow to sew, and we could really use your help with watching her."

Mother always knew how to keep Becca around. If it had been any other Saturday, she might have found an excuse to be busy, but with the plan to take pictures, she agreed. This might be the last time she would even see Tilly and her sweet niece.

"I can do that. I was thinking about taking pictures tomorrow anyway."

"Oh, now that's a good idea. Taking pictures always makes me happy. Tilly will be happy to see you too. You're going to have so much fun being an Auntie." Becca fought back heaviness as the words sunk in. She would not be around to be the Auntie.

Standing, she said, "I need to go see if I have film for the pictures."

Anger rose with every step she took upstairs. It was the stupidest thing. For her to be able to choose her life, she had to leave her family.

This is so stupid! This is so stupid!

By the time she reached her room, a full-blown anger attack had begun. To ease the emotion, she took a pen and started to make a list of all the names of her siblings, so she wouldn't miss anyone. In all, she counted eighteen.

***

Motivated by her picture-taking plan, Becca got up extra early the next morning and fixed her hair just right. Instead of secretly taking pictures, Becca made it very public as she found her siblings, posed them with props and had them say, "Cheese!"

Arlinda and Arnella were put together, of course, which was perfect because they had chosen to wear their pink checkered dresses again. Becca couldn't help but giggle. Younger children had it made.

Some of the middle children like Janessa and Justin were just random shots of tying shoes or playing. Because they were more aware, she had to be careful with her older siblings, so they wouldn't become suspicious of her motives and ask questions. Moving from room to room, Becca caught faces with her camera until someone yelled from downstairs, "Tilly's here."

Tilly was still standing in the entryway with a bundled, red-cheeked Danica when Becca stepped into the kitchen. Motherhood seemed to sit well with her. Since having Danica, Becca had also noticed Tilly seemed happier with Wally who appeared to be a good dad.

On occasion, Becca had even imagined someday she could find a way to like him too. After all, it wasn't his fault the prophet placed them in marriage.

"Here, let me get a picture," Becca said nudging her sister forward.

"I'm not ready," Tilly hesitated, smoothing her braid with her hand.

"You look fine," Becca countered with the camera resting on her hip.

With a half-hearted smile, Tilly posed, and Becca Clicked.

Satisfied, Becca added, "That wasn't too bad, now was it?"

The half-hearted smile gave way to a bright grin, and Tilly admitted, "It's nice to see you happy."

Touched by her kind words, Becca forced a silly grin and reached out for the baby, "Of course I'm happy, I get to play with my niece."

The day zoomed by. Tilly and Mother sewed as Becca tended Danica and snapped pictures until it was time for Tilly to go home. By dinnertime, Becca had filled two thirty-six strips of film. With a great sense of accomplishment, she walked upstairs, ready for some sleep.

Approaching her bed, she noticed another letter on her pillow. It was from Tilly. Her heart sank. There was no way anyone knew what she was planning, but it felt like everyone was trying to be super sweet to change her mind. She had painstakingly held smiles and tried to project a right attitude for the past week to guard herself against this very thing.

Sighing, she sat on her bed and began to read:

> My Dear, Sweet Sister, Becca,
>
> I feel so very privileged to be related to someone as neat as you. I love you so much and I'm counting on you to always be there for me whenever I need a friend. My children are also counting on you to be their favoritest Aunt Becca. Danica really does think you're pretty wonderful, and as she grows up she's going to be always wanting to go do stuff with her Aunt Becca. I just remember how we were with our Aunts, and how we still are with some of them...

It went on for three pages. The words were kind and genuine, but for some reason, anger was the only emotion Becca could allow.

Anything else would unravel it all.

18

A CODE OF HER OWN
MARCH 2002

CODE OF CONDUCT: PRIESTHOOD

The wicked will be wiped off the earth soon. Only those who have worked to create heaven on earth will be rescued from destruction. If young people want to be a part of heaven on earth, then they will have to set aside the ways of the world. Only the priesthood way of life can protect them. Otherwise, they will be left behind.

"Lighten up! You look like someone spit in your soup! And quit messin' with your hair, there's no way it can ever look as perfect as mine," Desiree teased as the three girls fussed in the tiny mirror at the photo studio.

"What? My hair always looks better than yours," Becca countered, and Desiree rolled her eyes. It was the truth, and she knew it.

"You've been so serious all day," Rachelle confirmed.

"Oh, I'm just nervous because we're gettin' pictures in our pants," Becca fibbed. It was a fact she didn't feel comfortable in them, though. Without the coverage of her dress, she felt like everyone could see the outline of her bottom. That was just plain weird.

Both girls looked up and giggled.

"You're such a nerd. We won't ever show this one to anyone. This one is just for our boyfriends and us," Desiree winked.

With all that she was, Becca longed to tell her best friends everything. By this time tomorrow, she would be living at her dad's. But she knew better. Nothing could cloud her focus now. If they knew about her plan, they might, in love, go to their parents out of concern and tell. Worse, they might get sad and try to talk her out of it. Neither of those two options was good. The letters from Jerusha and Tilly had been enough.

Wrapping one arm around Desiree and the other arm around Rachelle, Becca turned them to look in the mirror together, "Dang, we do look good in pants!"

"Now that's what I'm talkin' about!" Desiree said as she crossed her eyes and Rachelle stuck out her tongue.

"Let's go do this, dorks," Becca proclaimed, and they went to take their last pictures together.

***

"Don't you wish you looked as good as me?" Desiree pointed to the computer screen.

"You wish!" Becca snickered as the photographer showed them their photos and the girls decided which ones to purchase. They had changed several times, just as they had planned. In one grouping they wore jeans, another was in frog-printed pajamas, and of course, one was in their regular dresses, so they could show their parents.

Once all the pictures were printed, paid for, and dispersed, the girls went out to eat. Becca's high from the feeling of freedom was contrasted by feeling like an outsider once again. She listened to Desiree and Rachelle make plans for the Harvest festival. They wanted to sew matching dresses for it. Guilt had invaded earlier for not telling them, but as they planned, she knew Desiree and Rachelle would be ok. They had each other. And she would have Mac, her dad, and most importantly, her future.

On the drive back to the Crick, Becca carefully combed through the details of the next few hours in her mind. Most of the remaining items she intended to pack were already placed under the leopard print blanket on her bed. Those items would be put into a bag once everyone was asleep. She had also spoken to her dad on the phone at work that morning. He had talked to Mac. The plan was all a go. Not even a call from Uncle Warren would stand in her way at this point.

It was too early to feel relief, though. The next few hours of chores, dinner, and family prayer would be the last time she would probably ever spend with her whole family.

***

Becca looked around her bedroom that now felt odd. She had procrastinated as long as she could to avoid the last thing she needed to do: Write her Mother a note. Picking up her notebook and a pen, she sat down on her bed, and began to write:

> Dear Mother,
>
> I can't live here anymore. I know I can't be the perfect daughter you want me to be. I know you might feel like this is all your fault and that you haven't been a good mother. You have done and been everything a mother can be to her children. You've taught me so much. I have many of your awesome examples that so many people don't have. I love you so much for that. Love you forever.
>
> Your daughter,
>
> Becca

There. It was done. Purposefully, she had kept it short and general. Any deeper emotion would be too much. There was no way to explain how much she didn't want to have to be choosing between her family and her life. Her Mother just would not understand.

Perched on the edge of her bed in her purple Froggy pajamas, she contemplated the wait. This time would be like no other. Wired with restless energy, she would rather be doing anything other than sitting still but couldn't risk a conversation or interaction with anyone. Even Jerusha. She decided to just lay down until Jerusha was in bed, and then go lay on the couch outside of Mother's room. That way she could know when her Mother's lights were out, and all was quiet.

Laying still, waiting, Becca tried to remember all the things that had happened which led her down the path of choosing to leave. Envisioning Tilly's face, stained with tears as she stood in her wedding dress, Becca shuddered. Remembering Levi's insensitive words about his bride, her anger was fueled. Then, the shock of discovering Mac's sister sitting beside her stepfather was the last straw. Knowing of their marriage had cracked her faith in the idea of the Prophet's choosing completely. She remembered her cousin at the Golden Circle who she had been afraid of serving because he was an apostate.

She would be him now. At least she would be free to discover her own self, get to know her own dad better, and maybe even marry Mac.

After what seemed like hours, Jerusha went to bed, and the house grew quiet. Becca got up and stepped into the hall to lay on the couch outside her mother's room. Her light was on, so it would still be a while. Taking a deep breath, Becca laid down once more and covered up with her blanket. Moments later, her mother's door opened, and Becca's heart stopped.

"Oh, Becca, I was just going to check on you," she whispered, "what're you doin' out here?"

Becca pretended to be asleep. She didn't want to talk. Her mother sat down on the edge of the couch and touched her forehead, then placed a concerned hand on her back. Feeling her touch made her flinch, and she involuntarily opened her eyes.

"Oh, you're awake," Mother started.

"MMMM," Becca mumbled sleepily and turned to face the wall.

"Oh, Becca, you've been so distant and angry lately. I hate to see you this way. Yesterday you seemed happy for a while, and that made me so happy..." she paused.

"Tell me what you are thinking. Tell me what's going on. I feel like I'm losing you."

Becca gritted her teeth. It was precisely what she had tried so desperately to avoid.

"Just tell me what you're thinkin' like you used to. Please just talk to me Becca," she continued, her voice cracking.

Freshly fueled by remembering all her reasons to leave, Becca resolved to stay quiet. Keeping things from her mother never gave her pleasure. It went against her natural way of telling things the way they were. But this was not a time to tell it like it was. It would only wreck her plan and not convince her mother at all.

Her mother continued to speak, and Becca continued to pretend to be asleep.

After getting nowhere, her mother finally said, "I love you, Becca."

"Love you too," Becca mumbled as if she were drifting off without a care in the world. Except her world was disappearing. Even her heart seemed to stop as she held her breath waiting for the moment to pass. It wasn't that she was cold and unfeeling. It was that she felt too much all at once.

For a fraction of a second, she wondered if leaving was a huge mistake. She even reconsidered the Canada plan that had briefly brought her the hope of being able to marry Mac and stay in alignment with the church and her family. But she had tried that. No one would listen. It could only be one way or the other.

Finally, her mother retreated to her room and turned out the light. When all was dark, Becca's heart began to beat again. Even the night she had heard the coyotes in the distance surrounding her paled in comparison with the last minutes with her mother.

When it was safe, Becca slipped back to her own room, gathered the last things from under the blanket, and put them into her bag. She carefully set the note on her nightstand, folded the blanket, propped it onto the top of the bag, and lifted the bulky package.

On her way out, several dainty bottles of perfume stood lonely on her dresser, begging to come along. But she couldn't pack one more item. Maybe Jerusha would enjoy them, she hoped.

It was her last time to walk past her mother's room, down the stairs, through the kitchen, and out the side kitchen door.

Fighting the urge to run, she almost marched her way down the road. Her bag was uncomfortably awkward to carry with the blanket on top, and she didn't want to fall. Approaching the Spud Pit, it was dark and absent of the shadow of Mac's truck. She was late. Surely, he would have waited.

Her mouth went dry. Surely, he would show. Horrified, she began to panic. Everything had been put into motion. A small part of her worried that he may have left or been caught by the police for coming back into town. She imagined having to run back home, put the note away, and wake up the next morning with everything the same. If that was the case, then Uncle Warren could call. A dress could be made.

Unable to keep still and wait, she decided to walk toward the main road. To her relief, two familiar head lights appeared. It was him. Once the truck stopped and he opened his door, she nervously threw in his blanket and said, "This is for you."

Smiling, he took it sheepishly. "Did everything go ok?"

Eager to feel the relief of some miles between her and her family, she climbed into his truck and said, "Pretty good. My mother tried to talk to me. It was hard. But I'm better now."

Mac turned on the radio, and they traveled in silence for several miles. Becca allowed a little comfort and propped her feet up on the dashboard. It was peaceful until she looked out the side mirror and noticed red and blue flashing lights behind them in the distance.

"Mac, I think we're being pulled over," she almost whispered.

"Yep, looks like it," he said looking into his rearview mirror.

"Did we do something wrong? Do you think mother found my note and sent them to find us? What are we going to do?" Becca panicked. It was almost too much for her body to handle.

How could they know so soon?

"Just hang on. I was speeding a little, don't worry. Just let me do this," he assured.

Becca took her feet off the dashboard and sat statue-like as the officer walked over to her side of the truck and shined a light in, almost blinding her eyes. To her relief, she noticed he was not anyone from the Crick. That was a good sign.

"Can I see your license and registration?" he asked politely enough.

"Got it right here," Mac said and handed him the paperwork. The officer looked at the papers in silence and then gave them back.

"Do you know why I pulled you over?" he asked.

"I was driving a little fast," Mac offered.

"Yes, you were. Where are you going in such a hurry?" the officer prodded.

"I'm going to see my Dad in Riverton," Becca blurted.

Switching his attention to Becca, the officer said, "You look awful young to be up this late. How old are you?"

"I'm almost nineteen," Becca said.

"Well, you look more like fifteen to me," he said, surprised. "Do you have an ID?"

Trying to keep calm, Becca pulled out her driver's license and handed it to him.

Taking the license, he said, "There's a curfew, you know." Glancing at the ID, he continued, "Huh, you are eighteen."

The officer looked at Mac, then Becca, and said, "I'm going to let you off this time. You need to slow down and drive safe. These roads can be difficult this time of night."

"Thank you," Mac said putting his paperwork in the glove box.

"Thanks," Becca whispered.

"Be safe," he said and tapped the side of the truck.

"Ok," they replied in unison.

Brick-like, Becca sank into the chair. It took a bit, but after about twenty miles she started to feel like she could relax again. Occasionally, she checked the mirror for flashing lights.

"Do I really look like I'm fifteen?" Becca asked.

Mac laughed, "Well, you do look young compared to people off the Crick."

"Well, if I do, then you do too!" Becca teased.

Mac put his hand over her hand and said, "It's ok, we got this."

"I know," she said, squaring her shoulders.

In the morning she would be able to see him face-to-face by the light of day for the first time without fear of being caught. There was no longer a need for flashlights or codes. She could figure out how to listen to her own heart more freely and make her own decisions.

Good or bad, they would be hers alone to make.

And that gave her great comfort as she repeated his words, "We got this."

AFTERWORD

Most fiction ends, and the reader imagines the rest of the story. *The Crick Code* is different because, although we have changed most names, elaborated conversations, and compressed events to move the plot forward as a novel, it is based on Brenda's(Becca's) memories and documents which were collected along the way.

Throughout this project, I(Betsy) have been asked the same question: What happened after she left?

Life. Real life happened. Just a few weeks shy of her 19th birthday, she and Nate(Mac) were married. Those first years were a mixture of naïve love and isolated heartbreak over the loss of her family and friends. Shortly after their marriage, Brenda became pregnant with their first son and parenthood ensued. Wanting to share their son with his grandparents, Brenda and Nate took a day trip to the Crick. They visited, but had to stay outside.

Her beloved friends wrote letters, and some came to visit. Her mother and sister wrote letters for a while, but in September of 2002, Uncle Rulon, the prophet died, and that changed too. Warren Jeffs took over as Prophet and instated all kinds of new rules for the people to follow. One of which forbade true followers from corresponding with apostates, even through the mail.

In 2005 Warren Jeffs was indicted on felony charges of arranging a marriage between a 28-year-old man and a 16-year-old girl. Over the next few years, several allegations of under-aged marriages, and molestations substantiated with proof flooded the news. At one point he was even a fugitive.

After he was caught, convicted, and sentenced to prison, many of his faithful followers refused he had done anything wrong. Along the way, anyone who questioned his innocence or the way the church was being handled was kicked out. Each time they were declared apostates and another family was fractured. To date, Warren Jeffs still has a group of followers who are awaiting his release.

As of 2018, Brenda and Nate have been married for 15 years, have 4 children and own a successful family business. Every Christmas Brenda sends a family picture to her Mother, hoping she will see her grandchildren.

As the years passed, many of Brenda and Nate's friends, siblings and other family members left the Crick to make lives of their own. Only two of Brenda's blood siblings remain at the Crick. Several relatives who once shunned them have now been shunned themselves. Brenda and Nate hold no ill will towards them.

Brenda and her dad remain close.

Printed in Great Britain
by Amazon

48980870R00129